Edward Alfred Martin

Glimpses Into Nature's Secrets

Or, Strolls on Beach and Down

Edward Alfred Martin

Glimpses Into Nature's Secrets
Or, Strolls on Beach and Down

ISBN/EAN: 9783337030544

Printed in Europe, USA, Canada, Australia, Japan

Cover: Foto ©Andreas Hilbeck / pixelio.de

More available books at **www.hansebooks.com**

GLIMPSES

INTO

NATURE'S SECRETS;

OR,

STROLLS ON BEACH AND DOWN.

BY

EDWARD ALFRED MARTIN.

LONDON:

ELLIOT STOCK, 62, PATERNOSTER ROW.

1890.

PREFACE.

A DESIRE to do something towards feeding the widespread demand for information concerning the fascinating stories which Nature has to tell, is the plea which the author offers for the appearance of another work devoted to 'popular science.'

The first part is devoted to an attempt to bring under the observer's notice a few facts relating to those creatures of the sea-shore which, familiar more or less to all, are always replete with interest to the seaside sojourner, be he resident or visitor. It is hoped that the following chapters will be found neither too long nor tedious for those who seek but the elements of knowledge connected with the inhabitants of the shallows, nor too brief to obtain a satisfactory view of their chief characteristics; and that they may prove readable and entertaining, where lengthy and technical descriptions would be out of place.

In the second part the reader is familiarised with the study of the ancient history of our globe, as handed down to us in the form of rock-written stories, giving us glimpses of the various phases through which the earth has passed, and of the strange successions of animal life which from time to time, like a panorama, passed across the world's arena.

Most of the chapters contained herein have been contributed previously to the pages of various papers and magazines, and the author begs to thank the editors for their courtesy in permitting their reproduction.

That this collection of essays may act as a key to unravel some of the secret wonders of Nature, now hidden from so many, and that it may be the means of creating additional interest in the subjects dealt with, in the minds of those whose leisure hours are few, is the sincere wish of an ardent lover of Nature.

EDWARD A. MARTIN.

FOREST HILL,
1890.

CONTENTS.

PART I.

BY AZURE WAVES

CHAPTER I.

SOMETHING ABOUT A SCALLOP-SHELL.

CHAPTER II.

WHAT IS WATER?—HOW GEOLOGICAL STRATA ARE DEPOSITED.

CHAPTER III.

POWDERED WATER.

CHAPTER IV.

WHAT IS A SPONGE?

CHAPTER V.

A NOVEL USE FOR MUSSELS.

CHAPTER VI.

ABOUT CLAWS AND STONES.

CHAPTER VII.

A CHAPTER ON THE SEA-URCHIN.

CHAPTER VIII.

A FEW WORDS ABOUT THE STARFISH.

CHAPTER IX.

COMPOUND ANIMALS.

PART II.

ROCK-WRITTEN STORIES.

—◇—

CHAPTER X.

A RAMBLE OVER THE DOWNS.

CHAPTER XI.

A GEOLOGICAL JOURNEY FROM LONDON TO BRIGHTON.

CHAPTER XII.

A TALE OF TWO TEETH.

CHAPTER XIII.

THE GEOLOGICAL POSITION OF LONDON.

CHAPTER XIV.

NATURAL SCIENCE JOTTINGS FROM FELIXSTOWE.

CHAPTER XV.

A PIECE OF SANDSTONE.

CHAPTER XVI.

A FEW FACTS ABOUT THE ROMAN WALL ROUND LONDON.

PART I.

—◆—

BY AZURE WAVES.

CHAPTER I.

SOMETHING ABOUT A SCALLOP-SHELL.

Parasites—A Brazilian forest—Science begins at home—Chalk-covered worms — Protected by a sugar-loaf — The Sea of London —Acorn-shells—Dead-men's-fingers—A sea-flower— A Utopian Commonwealth.

HAVE you ever noticed the many peculiar growths which cover and thrive upon the exterior of the scallop shell? Some of them are most beautiful in shape and colour. Many an one has eaten dozens of scallops, at the same time heeding not in the slightest degree, perhaps, the brilliant artistic shell with which each individual has clothed itself, and the burden of parasites which it has been compelled to bear upon its back. They are instances of those many things which, so often present to our eyes, are yet invisible to our senses, at least until they are absolutely and specially pointed out to us.

There is a perfect colony of life growing upon a poor scallop's back, and indeed many a colony of colonies, for some individuals, as we shall see, are communities in themselves.

Let us purchase a specimen from the fisherman's barrow at our door, fresh from the ocean, and with its exterior plumage complete. We will neglect the scallop itself and pay our attention to one or two of the parasitical growths upon its shell. Truly wonderful parasites they are, too. Darwin speaks in one of his works of vegetable parasites, which, two feet in circumference, grow alongside of, and finally strangle, the enormous and luxuriant trees of a Brazilian forest. But the external growths of a scallop-shell are just as wonderful, and we need not go so far afield, but stay rather and search about upon our own seashore.

The first thing which will attract our notice are the many long worm-looking creatures, which wind and twist about in all sorts of contorted shapes over the surface of the shell. They look like worms which, when in the act of wriggling, had suddenly become petrified into long whitish chalky tubes of hard stony matter, so natural in form do they look. These tubes are the homes of little worm-like animals known as the *serpulæ*. They are found growing upon rocks, shells, stones ; in fact, upon anything which will give them a sure footing. An oyster will often be found actually covered by them. They collect from the water tiny particles of lime, and place atom to atom, as the bricklayer places brick to brick when building a house.

When living, a serpula is seen as a crown or tuft of

hairy processes projecting from the shelly tube. These hairy filaments are really the means by which it strains from the water the tiny bubbles of air which it breathes, each filament being provided with still finer hairs, or what are known as vibrating cilia.

When the little animal is obliged to place itself in a state of defence, it withdraws within its tube. Now, one of its breathing filaments carries at the end of it a structure in the shape of an inverted cone, or a sugar-loaf turned upside down. When the animal therefore feels so inclined it withdraws itself within its shelly tube, and, by the use of the conical plug, or *operculum* as it is called, it effectually closes itself to all comers. This is indeed a most wonderful and satisfactory means of protection for what might otherwise be so defenceless an animal.

Everyone is no doubt acquainted with the great bed of clay on which so much of London is situated, and which is known, therefore, as the "London Clay." This is proved by its fossil contents to have been deposited at the bottom of a fairly deep sea. The bed is as much as 500 feet thick, and whilst, therefore, this mass of clay was accumulating, the whole of the site of the great city was far beneath the waters of the sea. Now in the Sea of London these little animals, these same serpulæ, existed, just as their descendants do now on our coasts. In a similar way they then covered the oysters and other shells which existed in the ancient seas, and they are proved by their fossils to have lived in as great profusion as that in which they do now.

In close alliance to this animal is one which is just as familiar, being well known as the "acorn-shell," (*balanus*). This is also to be seen on our scallop's back, but not in such prolific numbers as when seen on the piles of bridges, etc. Look around the piles of any of the piers around our coasts when the tide is out, and you will at once notice, if you have not done so already, that the lower parts, which are covered at high tide by the water, are studded with a white chalky layer of tubercle-like shells, each perhaps a quarter of an inch in diameter. These are the acorn-shells, the abode of the little balani.

They are very similar in structure to the serpulæ, but instead of being closed by a plug, they possess two flaps of hard shell-like material which fall over and shut the little animal up within. When you examine the animal at low water, you will find, on looking in, that his shell-door is shut, and not till he feels or hears the water splashing about him will he open his door and extend his crown of tiny filamentous branchiæ to catch the still tinier animalcules which swarm in the water, and which form his staple food.

But now another interesting growth forces itself upon our attention. What are these indiarubbery masses of living flesh, which seem to cover so great a part of the shell of the scallop? Everyone must have noticed them. They are called 'dead-men's-fingers,' but they are no more dead when in their native element than the scallop itself.

They are generally of a bright orange colour, and they seem to us to have a texture something between that of a sponge and a piece of indiarubber. Zoologically they are of the family *alcyonidæ ;* order, *alcyonaria;* class, *actinozoa ;* sub-kingdom, *cœlenterata.* Now, to the actinozoa belong all the corals and sea-anemones, and indeed the dead-men's-fingers bear a great resemblance to both of these, although at first sight one would scarcely think so. The mass, as we find it on the scallop, is but the abode of the animal, just as the hard corallum is but the home, or, as in some cases, the back-bone of the coral polype (not insect, mind, for the coral is not an insect). The apparent difference then is simply in the style of architecture which each builds up.

They are often called ' compound animals,' because, in the case of the dead-men's-fingers, each little pore protrudes a flower-like animal, sometimes of brilliant colouring, and these are all organically connected with one another. It is as if one house contained them all, but each individual, having its own particular room, is tied down to that room, and can in no way interfere with its next-door neighbour. Everything which one eats benefits the whole community. No selfishness has a place there, no oppression of the weak, no ' survival of the fittest ' laws reign there ; what is good for one is good for all ; liberty, fraternity, and equality reign supreme, and thus in the lower animal kingdom we find that ideal commonwealth which man is continually striving for, but which, like an *ignis fatuus*, retreats the more as he thinks he approaches it.

CHAPTER II.

WHAT IS WATER?—HOW GEOLOGICAL STRATA ARE DEPOSITED.

Water — Its composition — Saltness of the Dead Sea — An
anemone's plight—A fairy's hand—How to make a salt-water
bath—Suspension—Solution.

SEE yon billow come bounding in with almost irre-
sistible force; see yon breaker dashing itself to
fragments on the stony beach. Look before you and see
the wide stretch of ocean, which extends far beyond
the reach of our narrow view, conjure up to your mind
the myriads of molecules of water which, rolling and
tumbling in loose contact with each other, go to make
up the vast expanse of the waters of the ocean; and
then bear in mind that every drop of water is composed of two gases united chemically in certain fixed
proportions, and that, therefore, the whole of the
visible ocean could be decomposed into *invisible* gases;
the sea then appears in a new light, as one of the
most wonderful phenomena of nature with which we

are familiar, and the contemplation of its inner invisible life serves perhaps to remove the apathy and
carelessness to its benefits which its constant presence
brings about in those who live permanently in proximity
to it. The gases of which *pure* water is composed
are hydrogen and oxygen. These are always present
in wonderfully exact proportions, viz., sixteen times
by weight of oxygen to two of hydrogen. Perfectly
pure water is, however, seldom found in a natural
state. Rain water which falls in the open country is
perhaps its purest form, that falling in towns being
contaminated by carbonic acid, ammonia, etc., which
are present in the air through which it falls, and which
it dissolves. But sea water, with which we are specially concerned, is water which has collected in the
lowest parts of the earth's surface, and towards which,
therefore, all water tends to flow from the higher
grounds. In the course of its flow it dissolves many
impurities, these being known to chemists as
'salts,' for although we apply the term 'salt' com-
monly to the ordinary table condiment, we must bear
in mind that there are many series of salts, far removed
from one another in point of composition, and that
common salt, or chloride of sodium, is only one of
many. We can therefore easily understand how
thoroughly salt a stream would become after traversing certain districts. The Dead Sea receives the
waters of the river Jordan and its tributaries, and with
them the scourings of the hills, to a great extent dis-

solved in them. The lake has no outlet. The sun, beating down on the surface, evaporates large quantities of water, but the salts remain behind, and as a consequence the water becomes more impregnated every year. This, as is well-known, is shown in a striking way by the buoyant properties of the waters of the lake as compared with those of fresh water.

A piece of cork, floating upon the surface of water, will bear a certain weight upon it ; so in a similar way many tiny molecules of salt dissolved in water will add materially to its buoyancy. The salt gives to water a higher specific gravity than that which it possesses when pure ; in other words, makes salt water to be heavier, bulk for bulk, than when it is in a pure state.

I remember, when a boy at school, having a living anemone in my possession. It had been captured at Black Rock, near Brighton. I wished to give it a change of sea-water, so proceeded to manufacture it, as I thought, by dissolving common salt in fresh water. Although this gave me *salt*-water, it certainly did not give me *sea*-water, and this the poor anemone soon found out. To make sea-water it would be necessary to prepare a quantity of each of those salts which are found in the sea, then to mix them up in the proportions in which they there exist, and finally to dissolve them in fresh water. Even then we might not get a satisfactory result, in consequence of the minute germs of life which are always present in sea-water, and which it would be almost impossible to transport.

But there is one way by which everybody might have a supply of very fair sea-water, and for which there would be no necessity to prepare one's own salt (or rather salts).

When crossing the channel, one very hot May day, as our vessel approached the French coast, we experienced somewhat rougher weather than that which had previously prevailed. Suddenly a large wave came along, drenching the deck with its spray. In a few seconds it had thoroughly dried up. But it had left something in its place. Look at the glistening and shining crystals which cover the deck where this wonderful tongue of the wave had kissed. Surely 'twas the hand of a fairy in disguise, which had raised itself from the ocean, to leave us such a beautiful deposit, reflecting and glancing back the rays of the mid-day sun! These crystals were the salts of the ocean which had been left in the moisture which had been deserted by the retiring wave. The sun's rays had greedily sucked up, by evaporation, all the moisture on the deck, and had left these crystals behind. Remove them quickly into a more shady place before old Sol returns to make another meal of them, and to cause them to disappear as rapidly as they came.

It will be seen, therefore, that should you wish to have a sea-water bath without bathing in the sea, it is only necessary to go down to the beach on a hot summer's day, take with you an ordinary tea-tray, fill it with a thin layer of sea-water, and leave it exposed to the rays of the sun. As soon as the water has evaporated, collect the salt left behind and refill with a fresh layer of sea-water. Collect after evaporation, and continue as long as perhaps your patience will allow you to do so. In this way 'sea-salt' can be had at a minimum of cost, and in a maximum of quantity.

It may be asked, if sea-water contains so much of these different kinds of salts, why are they not deposited in layers or strata at the bottom of the sea, in the same way as geologists tell us that strata of clay and sand are being laid down in our estuaries and seas, and as, for instance, the stratified rocks of the Weald and the Chalk Downs have been laid down in the remote ages of the past?

It is because water is capable of containing matter foreign to itself in two distinct ways.

When a stream running from a high to a low level is suddenly checked in its course, perhaps by its entry into a tranquil lake, it loses its force, and immediately matter is deposited at its entrance into the lake. This matter was simply held in *suspension* in the water, by reason of the velocity which the current possessed, but gradually sank as the stream lost that velocity. When matter previously held in this way in suspension is deposited, geological strata are formed.

But this is very different to the way in which sea-water holds its salts. They have been dissolved by the water, as sugar would be dissolved by a cup of tea, and are said to be held in *solution*, and whether the water be running or whether it be stagnant they remain dissolved (at least until the water containing them comes into contact with other bodies for which they have a greater *chemical* affinity than they have for water, when, uniting chemically with the new body, they are often precipitated).

Because the salts are held in *solution*, then, by sea-water they are not deposited, but mud and sand *are* deposited, because these are only held in *suspension*. When, however, the water of sea-water is removed by evaporation caused by the sun's heat, the salts are chemically precipitated, and these again may be dissolved in fresh water when required for bathing and other purposes.

The sand on the shore of a chalk district had been held in *suspension* by the sea when being ground down and transferred as flint from the chalk cliff, but the flint itself was no doubt held in *solution* in the sea of the chalk age, and precipitated in the fissures and crevices of the chalk where we now find it, perhaps in a similar way to that process now going on in Iceland, where the geysers deposit the crystals around their basin while the water is passing off in the shape of steam.

Sand, then, is simply mechanically deposited from suspension. Flint, on the other hand, is the representative of precipitation from solution.

CHAPTER III.

POWDERED WATER.

Ducks and drakes—Explanation—The oyster—A delicacy?—
Nineteen dozen a day—The maggoty-cheese eater—Pearls—
Natural causes—Vanity.

PURE water when in small quantities is an almost
colourless liquid. In larger quantities it assumes
a pale bluish tint. Sea-water varies from a blue to a
deep green. Why, then, it may be asked, is foam
white?

If you pound transparent glass in a mortar, if you
crush loaf sugar, or even quartz crystals, the same
result occurs; transparency gives place to opacity;
the glass pounded assumes a chalky colour, and the
same thing results in the cases of the sugar and quartz
crystals. A sea wave, consisting of partially transparent
water, dashes itself to fragments on the beach, and
brings itself into a similar condition to that of finely
divided glass powder when crushed in a mortar. The
reason for this chalky whiteness, is, that instead of the

surface of the wave or of the broken glass being in one plane, and so reflecting the diffused light from that one plane, each little particle of glass or water into which the whole has been broken up reflects light from its own particular surface in its own particular plane; thus we have light reflected in every direction, and from the multiplicity of cross rays a confused mass of whiteness is produced. This then, is, why the foam of the sea is white.

I suppose every little boy and girl has played at ' ducks and drakes ' when staying at the seaside. It will not be out of place to attempt a scientific explanation of even such a childish amusement as this. A thin stone or slate, with somewhat of a flat surface at least on one side, is thrown parallel to the surface of the water at but a few inches above the surface. Acted on by gravity, which attracts everything towards the centre of the earth, the stone, which should be thrown with its flattest surface next to the water, sinks and strikes as if to enter it at a very acute angle. But the flat surface refuses to allow the stone to enter the water as it would have done had an angular projection first encountered it, and as a consequence, impelled by the force imparted to it by the thrower, it slides along and rebounds from place to place on the water's surface. And when does it sink? When the attractional gravity overcomes (1) the gradually diminishing force primarily given to it by the thrower; and (2) the slight sustaining power of the water itself. The higher the thrower stands from the surface of the water, the less successful the throw will be, and the less the number of times of rebound. This is owing to the fact that the stone, in falling to the surface, has more time to accumulate a velocity in sinking towards the surface of the earth, and thus the water surface has momentarily a greater weight to sustain than that of the stone itself, and in a moment it has sunk.

When the stone meets the surface, thrown from a low level, it gives the surface but a slight weight to sustain, because there it is subjected to a strong force propelling it forward ; but when that force is expended, nothing prevents it sinking but its broad flat surface, and this does not sustain it long. But why does a flat surface sustain it any length of time at all? For the same reason that a piece of cheese would offer little resistance if cut through by a thin string, whereas a thick one would encounter a good deal of resistance ; because, indeed, there is a greater area of resistance exposed to the water. A piece of slate, if placed vertically in the water, would sink like a shot ; but if placed on the water horizontally it would take a considerable time to sink.

Of all the many species of shell-fish that are found native on our shores, perhaps the oyster is as well known as any among them. The delicacy of its flesh, and the digestibility of the animal, cause it to be in great demand amongst invalids, and gourmands of weak digestion. One of the great drawbacks to acquiring a knowledge of the natural history of any particular animal is the feeling akin to disgust which one feels on eating for food one of those very animals which have formed, at some period or other, the subject of one's investigation. For instance, this esteemed delicacy does not taste half so pleasant when one recognises the fact that in eating a dozen oysters one disposes of twelve stomachs, twelve mouths, twelve nerve-ganglions, twelve hearts, and twelve livers—and who, I would ask, is satisfied with twelve oysters?

The oyster is perhaps the most digestible kind of food known, even more so than bread, which, by-the-bye, in certain forms is decidedly indigestible. It is most nutritious, but containing so small a quantity of nitrogenous matter it is necessary for a man to eat nineteen dozen daily, if he abstain wholly from other food, in order to obtain the necessary quantity of nitrogen. In each oyster one eats, too, the digestion is aided by the bile secreted in the oyster's liver.

Oysters are often cultivated in what are called 'parks,' and are most prolific, one oyster depositing spat to the extent of about two million individuals. These are, however, considerably thinned by numerous fish which prey upon the young oyster.

Some people are very fond of cheese in which maggots can be seen roaming about at large. Similarly oysters are bred in 'parks' of stagnant water, offensive with greeny matter, in order that what is virtually a fattening disease may be induced in them, and so brought into a prime condition for the table of the maggoty-cheese-eater and his kin.

The pearl-oyster, or pintadine, also claims our attention. Although belonging to the oyster family it is of a different genus altogether to that of the common oyster. Pearls are formed when the oyster is in what may be called a diseased state.

Most people have noticed the glossy, shining substance, iridescent with every colour of the rainbow, which is so often seen on the interior of many of the shells cast upon the beach. The animal secretes this elegant lining of 'nacre,' as it is called, by abstracting the lime which is contained in the ocean. In the pearl-oyster this nacre is familiar as 'mother-of-pearl,' and is a valuable article of commerce. It is secreted, however, by other shells than the pintadine, although perhaps not in such lavish profusion. It is found in good preservation on many fossil shells, especially on the ammonites of the Gault Clay, many good specimens of which are to be found in every collection. The nacreous lining can be obtained by dissolving away the rough outer shell by the action of an acid, or by a process of polishing.

When a grain of sand or of some foreign substance happens to intrude itself on the domain of the pearl-oyster it is a source of great irritation to him. He, or she, for an oyster is both male and female, having both sexes in itself, forthwith, instead of continuing to add to the nacreous lining of the shell, proceeds to secrete layer after layer of pearly matter around the irritating object, and so smoothes it over with a substance akin to itself. In this way a pearl grows, as many as 150 stones having been found in one oyster. This number is, however, exceptional, and far above the average. The Chinese, as is well known, are in the habit of introducing various objects into the shell of the living animal with the idea of procuring pearls of a certain shape; these soon become coated, and the shell assumes the appearance of a natural cameo.

Pearl-oysters are collected at the bottom of the sea by expert divers, who are able to remain under water from thirty to thirty-five seconds without taking breath. The continual strain undergone in their dangerous occupation plays havoc with the constitutions of the divers. They seldom live to old age, and often rise to the surface with the blood flowing from their ears and nostrils. At what a price of human life are the rich bedecked with jewels, and at what a cost, indeed, is the gratification of vanity purchased!

CHAPTER IV.

WHAT IS A SPONGE?

As we know it—As it lived—The skeleton—Its flesh—Amœba —Convenient organs—Ripple-marks—Fossils.

WE all know a sponge when we see it, and can well appreciate its usefulness when we take (as everybody should whose health can bear it) our cold morning bath. We have often seen a small specimen of a sponge attached to the shells of scallops when they are in season. I wonder if as many know what the animal itself is, how it lives, of what it consists, and how it procures its food.

Just the same as our body consists of two essential parts, the skeleton and the flesh, so does the sponge consist of the same two parts, the horny skeleton and the sponge-flesh.

The sponges with which we are so well acquainted are only the skeletons of *Spongidæ*. What then was the animal part? It consisted of a layer of jelly-like substance (sarcode), which lined the skeleton within and without.   Everybody knows how a piece of sponge is perforated by numerous apertures and canals extending through and ramifying the mass in every direction.   The layer of sponge-flesh covered the horny skeleton and extended through all these ramifications which we have noticed, giving life to every portion of the mass, and using the skeleton as its support.

Then, again, what is the sponge-flesh ?

On invoking the aid of the microscope we find that the flesh is composed of a number of very little Amœbæ clustering together, and forming a colony. The Amœba, as you remember, is one of the lowliest representatives of life on the earth.   It is nothing but a little drop of jelly or albumen endowed with life. It possesses no mouth, but can conveniently make one in any part of its body near which its food may approach ; it has no arms, but can suddenly manufacture one in any part that it pleases, wherewith to seize its still more tiny prey.   For a heart it has what is known as a contractile vesicle, which does duty in its stead.

Well, a sponge is an assemblage of these Amœbæ. The single Amœba is enabled to roam about at will, and procure its food.   The sponge colony, however, is rooted to the rock, so its food has to be brought to it. This end is obtained by an interesting structure in the sponge.   Some of the flesh particles within are provided with little hair-like protuberances.   These being constantly vibrating, currents are set up in the water canals with which the skeleton is perforated, and in this way particles of food are brought within reach of the stationary colony, by an apparatus which in the free-swimming Amœba would be unnecessary, simply because it is able to go in search of its own food.

We see, then, that the sponge of everyday use is only the half of the original structure. Most people will agree that it is the better half. For although albumen, of which its flesh is composed, is all very well for food in the shape of white-of-egg, I am not aware that anybody has at present suggested taking the albumen of the sponge, and using it for the many purposes of cooking to which eggs are put.

A peculiar fact, however, is that what appear to be shapeless little Amœbæ are to be seen in the blood· which flows through our veins. There they throw out their little arms, or pseudopoda, in every direction, and roll and tumble about just the same as their relatives do outside their human home.

Everybody has noticed the ripple-marks that are found on the sands at low water. They seem as though tiny waves had come rippling in and had suddenly become petrified into sand-ridges. Now although man has lived but a short time, comparatively speaking, on this earth of ours, yet, by the aid of researches into the formation of the rocks beneath us, we are able to go far back in the history of our planet; we can arrive at a period so remote from now,

as to be long anterior to that when the human race
first made its appearance, and there in the sands
which were to be found at the bottom of the Carboniferous sea, and which have since been consolidated
into hard sandstones, you would have found just the
same action of the sea making ripples, in exactly the
same manner as it does now. So the physical action
of the sea went on in those days regardless of the
changes which were going on around, and sub-
mitted the sands to the same process as that which
it does now, in a world of living beings so different to
that now existing, that were a Carboniferous human
being to come to life now, had such an one ever lived,
he would find himself translated to an entirely different
sphere to that to which he had been accustomed.
·What is more, we find that the sea sand-ripples
became so hardened that when they were covered up
by a fresh layer of sedimentary matter, they retained
their shape, and now, after the flow of ages not to be
counted, we dig up in our quarries slabs of stone
covered by ripple-marks, reminding us that we are
walking over an old shore of sand, in a district, perhaps,
where the sea has not washed for many hundreds of
years. Some beds of sandstone are covered in every
layer by these fossil ripple-marks, and are often used
as tiles for the roofing of houses.

Ripple-marks are found in other formations ; in the
Wealden Beds in Sussex, at Horsham, Cuckfield, etc.,
they occur very frequently ; in some of the slabs of

sandstone of which our pavements are formed we have often noticed the same peculiarity (we must not, however, mistake for it the diagonal cuttings made in the stones in order to prevent the foot slipping). When we next tread upon an uneven curbstone, let us just give it a glance, and we will see if we can recognise these ripple-marks.

CHAPTER V.

A NOVEL USE FOR MUSSELS.

A silk-spinning shell-fish — Living cement — Wood-borers — Sussex coal — Lignite or brown coal — False hopes — The Brighton Spa.

EVERYBODY is acquainted with the mussels which are seen clustering at the ends of the groynes at our seaside towns. They are always to be found, at low tide, clinging tightly to the wood or iron to which they have attached themselves. Go and watch them when the tide is coming in, and see the waves dashing against them, and threatening every moment to sweep them away. I used to wonder how they could possibly withstand the force of the waves, sufficient oftentimes to knock a human being off his feet. Dislodge a few mussels, and place them in some sheltered spot where the force of the waves is not the strongest. In a few days they will once more be found to have taken root, and to offer considerable resistance to being again removed. Why is this?

It is because of the power which the mussel possesses of spinning a silk-like web, or *byssus*, by which it is enabled to cling so tightly to the groynes and the rocks as to resist the ordinary force of the waves in their efforts to remove it. This binding power which the mussels have is by no means useless. When the French engineers set to work on the breakwater at Cherbourg, they invoked the aid of the mussel to assist them. Tons of mussels were transplanted and placed upon the works. To protect themselves from being swept away they spun their *byssus*, and let go their natural anchor, in this way uniting themselves firmly to the blocks which formed the breakwater, and also to each other. Thus, blocks and mussels were firmly bound together; and while the mussels congratulated themselves on having withstood the force of the waves, the engineers congratulated themselves on having obtained, at a very cheap price, a firm, though living, cement, in the shape of the poor unconscious mussels.

Have you ever noticed how closely the wooden piles of the Chain Pier at Brighton are studded with iron nails, and has it ever occurred to you to ask the reason of it? Do the nails strengthen the structure? Well, they do, in an indirect way.

There are some terrible little creatures existing in our waters who are exceeding fond of cosily burying themselves in a comfortable nest of wood. These animals are not much to look at, but they have proved themselves to be of alarmingly destructive habits.

They are known as the (i.) *Pholas*, or 'piddock,' and
(ii.) *Limnoria terebrans*, a very insignificant animal
indeed, but one greatly to be dreaded. The latter,
scarcely an eighth of an inch in size, eat their way
into any wooden piles that may be immersed in sea-
water, and thus open the way for a more terrible
pest, viz., the 'ship-worm' (*teredo*). When it was
found that the piles of the Chain Pier were suffering
from the ravages of these little monsters, heads were
placed together to find out a way by which to outwit
them. To encase the piles in iron would have been a
somewhat expensive job, so a plan was hit upon to
cover them with broad-headed nails of iron, placed so
closely as to allow of no entry for the little bore.
Though able to burrow into wood, iron proved itself
their match.   Hence the reason for the coat of
armour which the piles appear to wear.

Every now and again large lumps of a brown-
black material are washed up on the beach in front of
the town of Brighton. These are of all sizes, from a
rounded fragment of a few inches thick to large slabs
of it. It is really a kind of coal. If it had not been
tossed about by the sea so unmercifully, but had
remained in its former place of deposition, in the
course of time it would most likely have become true
coal. It has assumed the rounded shape in consequence of the continual action of the sea having worn
off the jagged corners, and this is also the reason that
we scarcely ever find a single stone on the beach

which possesses a sharp edge. The continual attrition
of the flints, one with the other, after they have been
washed out of the chalk, has chipped off and
rounded the edges, and the tiny pieces so broken off
have gone to be pounded still smaller into sand ; thus
we might form a collection of beach-stones, and,
arranging them according to their size, show that the
boulder and the grain of sand are but the extreme
gradations of one and the same series. This lignite,
as it is sometimes called, or, as it is better known,
surturbrand, was used at one time by the fishermen
for burning as fuel. It, however, gave out such an
offensive sulphurous odour that a by-law was passed
prohibiting the fishermen from using it.

It had its origin in the beds which formed the
Brighton Cliffs, when they were exposed to the action
of the sea, and before the Cliff Formation was hidden
behind a wall of concrete. Now, however, it is to be
found in the shape of a bed of lignite running under
Furze Hill. Sir Roderick Murchison paid a visit to
this deposit in 1850, and mentioned it in his writings
as being impregnated with iron pyrites (iron sulphide)
and giving rise to the neighbouring Chalybeate of
Wick. Bright indeed were the hopes that were raised
that this lignite might prove a veritable coal-mine, but
they were only to be dashed to the ground, even as
those which were raised concerning the lignite of the
Wealden sands at Bexhill. Mr. Montague Phillips
stated that he traced the Furze Hill lignite for a dis-

tance of 1,370 feet, south to north, and it was doubtless formerly connected with similar beds at Newhaven
and Bognor.

In many pieces of surturbrand that have been cast
up, as also in chalk boulders that have been in the
water some time, we find the ravages of our friends
the borers, but this time it is the work of the *teredo
navalis*, or ship-worm.   These perforations will be
found to have been made as a rule in parallel directions, literally riddling the substance which has been
bored.   His companion borer, the *Pholas*, bores in
all directions, having no hesitation in crossing his
neighbour's path, without even asking his permission,
or begging his pardon.

Fossil wood is found plentifully in the London Clay,
bored in a very similar manner by a species of the
ship-worm, and doubtless those which infest and de-
stroy the timbers of ships and piers in the present day,
are direct lineal descendants of those which ages ago
found their snug homes in the heart of the wood
which grew in the tropical forests of the Eocene age.

CHAPTER VI.

ABOUT CLAWS AND STONES.

A fishwife's belief—It would not grow—Flint crystals—The worse for wear—Natural assortment of the beach and sand.

THERE was once an old woman who lived by the sea, who earned her livelihood by the sale of small lobsters, crabs, and other shell-fish which she picked up on the sea-shore. One day her little boy met with a misfortune. By some means or other one of his fingers had been chopped off, and he went home crying to his mother. The doctor was interviewed, the boy's hand was bandaged up, but the mother became impatient with the slow progress the finger made, and, visiting the doctor a second time, gravely informed him that the finger 'had not yet begun to grow again.' Now the old woman was evidently mistaking the zoological characteristics of *homo sapiens*, or the human being, for those of *homarus vulgarus*, the common lobster. Most people are aware that the lobster, when it loses a limb, has the power of producing another one in its place. This power of re-production is not confined to the lobster, but is common to other crustaceans. If a lobster can grow a fresh limb in place of a lost one, thought the old woman, why should not her boy's finger grow again in a similar fashion?

She was reasoning from analogy, but analogy played her false.

If one were to take a ramble along the shore and make a collection of nothing but various kinds of stones, a very interesting number of varieties would be found. The great body of stones and pebbles one finds on the beaches around the south coast are derived from the bands of flints which intersect the chalk cliffs. Rolled and tossed by the ocean, they have been worn into their present rounded forms, varying from those of the size of a pea to large heavy boulders. Flints are composed of a substance known to the chemist as *silica*. Many of the most valuable of our precious stones are composed of exactly the same material, for instance, amethyst, onyx, cat's-eye, etc. Quartz also has the same chemical composition, so that we see that the common substance known as flint has an exact similarity of composition with that of some of the rarer stones. Who, too, has not found occasionally in the heart of a stone, a beautiful crystallized centre? These crystals have been prepared in Nature's own laboratory from the surrounding mass of flint.

A good instance of the action of the sea in round-ing off all rough corners and edges, met me a short time since, when at Brighton. I found a piece of whitish granite that had been washed up by the sea, with its edges all rounded off. I should have liked to have thought that it had been washed up Channel from, perhaps, the granite cliffs of Devon or Cornwall. A closer inspection, however, showed that it possessed exactly the same texture and composition as that possessed by the granite which the workmen had used in building the Hove Sea-Wall. It was, in fact, a piece which the labourers had chipped off, and which had been on its travels seawards, and had now returned to be cast up by the sea, decidedly 'the worse for wear.'

Another stone which I found had, I believe, no connection with any such works of masonry as the above. This was a pebble of *gneiss,* a rock which does not appear anywhere in the neighbourhood. Gneiss is a primitive rock, and is supposed to have been formed from the disintegration of granite. It possesses the same composition, viz., felspar, quartz, and mica, but instead of its crystals being disseminated irregularly in the mass, they have been deposited in regular layers by the action of water.

Thus a gneiss (pronounced *nice*) pebble would show its constituents arranged in regular stratula, and would at once be distinguishable from amorphous granite. This pebble having travelled so long a journey by the locomotive power of the sea, was

thoroughly rounded, and at first sight was not to be
known from an ordinary flint pebble.

It is interesting to note the way in which beach is
sorted by the sea. When in Devonshire last year, I
collected specimens of various sizes of pebbles from
the streams flowing from off Dartmoor. These
pebbles had been formed by the decomposition of the
granite. On shaking them all up together, I noticed
that the very small ones had sunk to the bottom,
while the larger ones lay upon the surface of the
rest. In this way the beach seems sifted and sorted.
We find, as a rule, the larger boulders furthest
removed from low-water mark, whilst next to them
appear those of medium size, gradually giving way,
as we approach the sands, to the very small beach.
Beneath them, we come finally to the smallest and
finest of all, viz., the sand, and this is composed of
exactly the same material as flints, but has undergone the most minute subdivision of all by the continual trituration caused by the waves.

CHAPTER VII.

A CHAPTER ON THE SEA-URCHIN.

A soft body—Radiating spines—Fossil urchins—Tube-feet and suckers — ' Hedgehog-skin ' — Ingenious power of growth — Shell composed of numerous plates.

THERE are many creatures inhabiting the sea with which we are, perhaps, more familiar than the sea-urchin, yet there are few of us who have not picked up specimens of the animal when at the seaside, or found some of its empty egg-shaped shells amongst the stones of the beach. It can be more successfully sought for after a storm, for then it has been forcibly removed from the deeper water which it finds more congenial to its tastes. When thus found it generally still possesses complete both the soft body inside, and the hard radiating spines attached to the shell outside. The flesh of some species is said to be in flavour not unlike that of an ordinary chicken's egg, and it is, therefore, sometimes known as the sea-egg. The flattened shape of most individuals, however, rather suggests a likeness to a crown or diadem than to an egg, and advantage has been taken of this to call a well-known fossil-urchin by the name of *diadema*, for, of course, we must remember that the ancestors of those now living existed in ages a long, long time ago. Most people have seen sea-urchins' shells which have been dug out of the chalk. Every museum collection has specimens of them, and in some cases they have become petrified both inside and outside, and now each one consists of nothing but a heavy lump of flint. The flint has taken the exact form of the animal, and we see the same markings on its shell as those which we see on the specimen just recently taken from the water.

The creature seems to be of a very harmless disposition, and yet it is obliged to wage merciless war upon its companions in the sea in order to supply its daily wants. Worms, crustaceans, and small molluscs constitute the principal portion of its food, and it seems to have a strange power of inducing a kind of paralysis in its prey, which it seizes by means of the tube-feet which we shall mention presently. An urchin was once seen to capture a small crab, and fixing its teeth and suckers into the soft parts of the animal, held it in a seeming state of paralysis until it became sufficiently weak to allow of the sea-urchin enjoying an uninterrupted meal.

Its shell and appendages are wonderful specimens of mechanism and architecture. On cutting the shell in half and looking at its inner surface, it is seen to consist of numerous regularly arranged plates, in shape something like a small domino with the four corners cut off, generally being octagonal in form. These plates are dovetailed into one another by their angular projections, but are arranged in vertical rows reaching from the summit to the mouth at the base of the shell. Five of the rows consist of large, and five of small plates, and these are arranged alternately with one another. Thus the shell is formed of ten vertical zones of plates, the manner in which they are arranged reminding one of the appearance presented by the surface on the school-globes, being divided into a number of zones by the meridians of longitude.

We will, first of all, deal with those zones consisting of the smaller-sized plates. If we take an empty shell and hold it in front of a bright light, we see that near the edges of each vertical zone it is perforated by a double row of tiny holes. Through these little apertures the animal, when alive, had the power of putting forth what are known as 'tube-feet'; these were well supplied with muscles, and each one carried at its extremity a sucker, by which it could cling tightly to the rocks over which it wished to pass. By this means it was enabled to pull itself forward in the direction required. In one case a sea-urchin was seen crawling up the perpendicular glass of an aquarium, such was the power of its suckers. As, too, the feet were well supplied with nerves, there is no doubt it could literally 'feel its way,' and so assist its eye-spots in surveying its path. The tube-feet are exceedingly numerous. In a specimen examined sixty holes were counted in the shell in each vertical row of plates. As there were ten double rows of holes, there could have been no less than 1,200 tube-feet which the creature was able to protrude; and in speaking of these we cannot but be struck with the similar power possessed by the tiny unorganized foraminifera, whose shells are perforated by numerous holes, through which they are able to protrude their little pseudopodia.

The living creature is assisted considerably, too, in its mode of progression by the spines to which we have before referred, and which are distributed over the exterior of the shell, especially on the large zones. The zoological class to which the creature belongs, viz., *echinodermata*, literally translated, means 'hedgehog-skin,' and this name conveys a very good impression of the appearance presented by the spine-covered shell of the sea-urchin. The spines project like the quills of a hedgehog, and are movable by special muscles attached to them. They are capable of a wide range of movement, being affixed to the shell by means of a 'ball and socket joint.' If you close the fist and spread your remaining hand closely over it, you have a very good illustration of what is meant by this, the closed fist representing one of the tubercles with which the shell is studded, and from which the spines project, the hand into which the fist fitted being the foot of the particular spine proper to it.

Add to these means of progression the fact that some of the spines terminate in a three-fingered prong which clasps the seaweed as the creature moves along, and it will be seen that it is not the stationary animal which it would appear at first sight to be.

As the animal grows with increasing years, it would almost seem that the brittle shell which encased it would break by reason of the pressure inside. It is, however, provided with the necessary power of growth to meet the requirements of the growing animal, and this power is a wonderful provision, which, in order to retain the egg-shape of the shell, allows of the growth of each individual plate of which its zones consist, by the deposition of calcareous matter at every edge, and, therefore, the contemporaneous enlargement of every portion of the shell. In the specimen referred to, each vertical zone consisted of forty hexagonal plates. There being ten zones, large and small, there must have been 400 plates which formed the shell. We can well understand how wonderfully the egg-shape of the shell is preserved by the gradual enlargement of each individual plate.

The sea-urchin can bury itself in the sand with the greatest ease, by means of its spines; and by the aid of the teeth, five in number, which surround the mouth, it is enabled to bore into the hardest rock, and, there ensconced, bid defiance to all pursuers.

CHAPTER VIII.

A FEW WORDS ABOUT THE STARFISH.

On its back—Ten rows of feet—-Its power of renovation when mutilated—Stars and comets—Sea-cucumbers—Lily encrinites.

THERE are few objects more common on the sea-shore than the five-fingered starfish, and no one can ramble along a quarter of a mile of coast without meeting, perhaps motionless and seemingly lifeless, this gaudy, orange-coloured, terrestrial star. Watch it for a few minutes, and unless it has been deserted by the tide for too long a space of time and has therefore become dried and stiff, you will most likely have the satisfaction of seeing it move. Its shape is very convenient for locomotion, as it can move off in any direction it pleases without having to turn itself about. Now, by what means does the creature move? Just as it is starting, suddenly throw it over on its face. You will at once notice a number of short worm-like tubes, which are continually feeling around as if trying to grasp something. These tubes, or *ambulacra* as they are called, bear a close resemblance to the tube-feet which we found protruding through the shell of the sea-urchin, and the manner in which they are used, and the source whence they come, are in both cases the same. On the shell of the sea-urchin, it will be remembered, we found ten distinct rows of tubes, which were pushed out from the holes in the shell. In the starfish we now find that its five rays are admirably fitted to receive ten similar rows; and when we turn the fish on its back we see that it has two of these rows on each of its fingers, one row on each side. It makes use of these tube-feet to move itself along, and we can see it struggling on its back, and waving its many feet to and fro in its vain efforts to right itself.

The feet are not always distinctly visible. When first turned over on its back, perhaps nothing is seen of them, and in their place appears only a shiny mass of jelly-like substance. Gradually, however, they become unfolded, and each assumes its worm-like form. How is this? It is because at the base of each foot there is a little globular-shaped sac, filled with a watery liquid, and each of these is connected with its neighbour. When the animal wishes to put out its little feet it causes all the little globular sacs to contract, and the result of this is that the watery liquid is forced into the feet, which then expand and stand out. When the sacs again enlarge, the liquid is withdrawn from the feet, so that they become limp, and droop into their former motionless condition.

The starfish is an inveterate enemy of the fisherfolk. It can strangely scent prey from afar, although no organs of scent or hearing have been discovered. When a bait is lowered into the sea it attaches itself to it, and the angler that finds he has taken the trouble to draw in his line only to find the five-fingers at the end of it, vents his anger on the animal by mutilating it, and, tearing it across, casts it back into the ocean. It will, however, bear this mutilation with equanimity, for where before it was but one fish, now there will be two. Each half will proceed to grow the requisite number of limbs it has lost, and enjoy two-fold its humble life. The lower we get in the scale of life the more pronounced do we find this wonderful power of reproducing a lost limb, or other organ. When walking on the sands at Felixstowe, I discovered a small starfish which had, young as it was, already lost one of its fingers, but a new one had commenced to grow in its place, and it looked somewhat comical to see the fifth only about half the length of the remaining four.

In some parts of the Indian Ocean it is common to find the fish producing four rays at the extremity of another, giving not so much the appearance of a star as of a comet. This may be partially owing to the fact that the stomach, which is situated in the centre immediately above the mouth, has prolongations into each of the arms, and each arm as it was torn off carried with it an accompanying portion of stomach. In other instances the arms themselves have subdivided into two shorter arms, and in such a case the symmetry of the star became of course lost. Specimens exhibiting this feature can be seen in the British Museum.

Although the starfish does not possess the hard shell-covering which protects the urchin, it also belongs to the 'hedgehog-skin' class. The skin, as everyone knows, is covered by a number of jagged pieces of lime, the spicules and spines, which give it a rough uneven surface, and which answer to the plates of lime which constitute the shell in the sea-urchin. Throughout the whole sub-kingdom, 'Echinodermata,' the animals are covered by these spicules and spines of lime, most completely in the case of the urchins, and least in *holothuroidea*, the sea-cucumbers, where they are scattered very sparingly over the skin.

The starfish is decidedly voracious, and can eat even oysters. When, however, it attacks one that is too large for its stomach, it inverts this organ over it, and is able to compel the mollusc to open its shell, when it easily falls a prey to its captor.

In times now long past, especially in the seas existing when our great coal-beds were laid down, a peculiar kind of starfish was abundant, which was fixed to the rocks by a stalk consisting of plates of bone. There it grew and sent out branches and twigs, each one ending with a beautiful long-fingered starfish. They are known as *crinoids* or encrinites, from the Greek word krinon, a lily, since when partially open they presented the appearance of a beautiful lily. These stalked starfishes were so plentiful in the seas that hundreds of them are now seen imbedded as fossils in the hardest rocks, and a number of different species have been discovered. Although then existing in such profusion, there are now living only two or three species of crinoids, so great has been the decrease that has taken place ; and perhaps, in a few hundreds of years, the family will have to be numbered with other animals which have become extinct since the appearance of human beings on the globe.

Of the starfish itself there are very many species living, and hence we may note there is but little possibility of their dying out for many ages.

CHAPTER IX.

COMPOUND ANIMALS.

Three great classes—Their names—A sea-fern—Its precarious
means of subsistence—The coral-builders—Fossil coral-reefs—
Sea-mat—It encrusts seaweed—It is highly organized.

THE creatures to which Linnæus applied the name
'animalia composita,' or compound animals,
constitute the great bulk of those which were formerly
known as zoophytes. A compound animal is an assemblage either of *polypites*, or of *polypes*, or of
polypides, these being the terms which have been
applied to the individuals of each of the three classes
which are made up of this kind of being. Of the first
two mentioned, many species are to be found on our
own sea-shores, whilst concerning the last, the polype,
it may safely be said that although we have not all
seen it in a living state, we have heard of the result of
its herculean labours in the banks of coral which it
has built up in various parts of the world, as well as in
the pretty red coral which is so much used in the

manufacture of articles of ornament. They are all known as compound animals, since when living they exist in colonies of many thousands of individuals, united to each other either organically, or by the mass of coral to the formation of which all are contributing their share.

But why, it may be asked, is a distinction made between them, and why the different names? It is because each of the three classes have organic structures which differ from those of the others, and which have compelled naturalists to separate them and to distinguish between the more highly and more lowly organized amongst them. To begin with the most humble of the three, we have not to go far in order to procure a species belonging to the great class HYDROZOA, whose single individuals are called *polypites*, for we must all have noticed the fern-like seaweed which grows on the backs of shell-fish, and which is invariably to be found on the shell of the well-known scallop. There it grows to a height of some five or six inches, sending out branches right and left, and looking not unlike the common garden fern with its leaflets. When examined it will be noticed that both edges of the stem and of the branches are cut up into something resembling the edge of a saw, so that between each part corresponding to its tooth there is a little cavity. In this species, one of the sertularians, each little polypite was situated in one of the cavities, so that when all were filled and the organism was complete, the colony consisted of a large body of individuals congregated together. Yet they were not individuals in every sense. Each one, though isolated and bound down to his little cell, was compelled to contribute to the maintenance of the whole colony. The food which it procured from passing currents, went to sustain the whole body, every individual being in organic connection with the rest by means of the horn-like substance which constitutes the only part remaining when the organism is dead. The polypite itself can well be imagined by taking the common anemone as a model, for, although it had not the same interior arrangements, there was a similarity in its means of obtaining food, namely, by the assistance of a number of tentacles, which engulfed the tiny infusores which came within their reach, and conveyed them to the central mouth.

In the *polype*, however, the individual peculiar to the class ACTINOZOA, we have a distinct advance in the organization of the creature. The term is applied to those individuals which go to constitute the colonies known as coral-builders. They are similar in external appearance to those of which we have just spoken, but differ from them in the enjoyment of a stomach distinct from their body-cavity.

The colossal results brought about by the continual labour of the coral polypes are seen in the numerous groups of islands which stud the Pacific Ocean, and in the extensive hidden coral-reefs which in some parts bound the shores of the great continent of Australia. Although we cannot, however, actually observe their work now going on in our own seas, we have ample proof of their presence in times past, for in some of our geological formations, such as, for instance, the Coral Rag of Oxfordshire, we encounter great banks of coral in a fossilized condition, which are as assuredly the works of polypes as those masses now being formed in tropical seas. So extensive are some of these fossil coral reefs, that they are broken up and used for road-mending ; indeed, so many limestone formations have been found to owe their origin to the working of various species of animalcules, that it has been hazarded by many eminent scientific men that, perhaps, there is no form of limestone, be it chalk, coral rag, or encrinital marble, that has not at some time or other formed part of an organized being, which has been left after death the tenantless hecatomb of a life that has passed away.

One is sometimes exercised to understand how it is that such apparently differing substances as the ordinary tree-like red coral, and the globular brain-shaped coral which is so often seen in cabinets and on mantel-shelves, can possibly be the production of animals of the same class. To understand this, it must be explained that there are two modes of coral formation, and the distinction is an important one to remember. What is known as red coral was really the internal stem of the animal, and during life it was surrounded by a thin rind of fleshy substance, similar to the manner in which the trunk of a tree is covered by a layer of bark. In this rind were situated the clefts which held the polypes, which were thus entirely isolated from the internal skeleton. In the massive coral, on the other hand, they were encircled by the calcareous skeleton itself, which even took the shape of the polype, and was secreted in the very organs of the animals themselves. Consequently, this kind of coral is full of small holes or clefts, and in these the creatures lived.

Thus the whole colony in both kinds was nothing but a congregation of minute sea-anemones, the internal organization being in fact the same as that possessed by them.

When we turn our attention to the third class, the POLYZOA, whose individuals have been termed *polypides*, we at once enter upon a much higher scale of organization than that possessed by either the Hydrozoa or the Actinozoa. There is one species common on our shores which serves well to illustrate this important class. Popularly it is known as the 'sea-mat,' technically as the *flustra*. Oftentimes it is cast up by the waves as a bunch of what is apparently seaweed, growing perhaps from a common root, and sending its leaves upward in the shape of thin ribbon-like stems, to a height of three or four inches. On the other hand, instead of forming stems of its own, it sometimes encrusts true seaweed with a thin layer of its cells, covering it in very truth with a 'sea-mat.' Its external appearance suggests that a number of indentations, called sacs, have been punched in the horny membranous tissue of which it consists. If examined under a microscope when alive, from each little sac à cluster of hairs is seen cautiously to come forth. Then, if the coast seems clear, the tentacles themselves creep out, and finally open and expand like a flower. The sacs which contain them seem to overlap one another like the scales of a herring, and at the extremity of each is the narrow slit or orifice from which the creature spreads itself out. Thus their whole external structure suggests an intimate connection with the other compound animals we have mentioned ; and, indeed, in the result of their labours, the building of their own houses, a great likeness is exhibited between them. The *flustra* differs, however, so widely from the other two classes, that it has been placed amongst the mollusca (*mollis*, soft), although forming a humble class in that sub-kingdom. Its high position is at once justified by the fact that, besides possessing the mouth and bag common to the sertularian, each individual possesses a gullet, a gizzard, and a membranous stomach, which is connected with the mouth by a distinct alimentary canal.

In conclusion, then, we find compound animals are of three classes, differing, indeed, widely in their internal organization, but similar in their external characters, in their precarious mode of subsistence, and above all in their mode of life, which allows of many thousands of individuals, although entirely isolated from each other, still to remain part and parcel of one great organism.

PART II.

—◆—

ROCK-WRITTEN STORIES.

CHAPTER X.

A RAMBLE OVER THE DOWNS.

The Queen of Watering-places—Her breezy Downs—Nature's
Fairy-tales—Southdown flocks—Shady woods—Denudation
of the chalk and overlying beds—River-drift man—Ditchling
Beacon—A living panorama.

TO those accustomed to look upon the town of
Brighton simply as a pleasant seaside suburb of
London, as a place of recreation wherein to recruit
one's wasted energies after the bustle and rush of
city life, very little appears to be known of the
country in the vicinity of the town, and the vast
opportunities offered, but lost, to those in search of
health and strength, who come to the town without
visiting the broad and breezy Downs which encircle
it on three sides, and which, with the bracing air
which rolls over them and the sense of freedom and
latitude that they impart to those who visit them,
help to give Brighton a high place in the list of
healthy towns.

Rambles over these pleasant hills will give both

health and pleasure, if one can appreciate Nature, silent yet grand, as exhibited to us in the wonderful Downs of Sussex and Kent; silent in the grandeur of the lofty rounded heights, grand in the sublime silence she now maintains from internal commotion after the destruction and denudation which she underwent in a past geological age ere she presented herself peaceful and quiet, a lasting evidence of the mighty forces over which she holds sway, and by which she works her wonders. How such a country ramble can be made interesting and entertaining is best known to those who possess a love for, and can appreciate Nature, in whatever branch of natural science his special liking may be.

To the ordinary pedestrian, who exercises his limbs by a walk across the Downs, nothing, perhaps, is noticed beyond gentle slopes and valleys, stretching as far as the eye can reach, and covered by a short thick herbage, affording excellent pasture-land for the rearing of the well-known Southdown mutton. The geologist takes his ramble, and though he be bent exclusively on geological research, he finds himself taking more and more interest in some kindred, yet entirely different science. He cannot follow his study of the fossils with which he may meet without, for instance, some acquaintance with the study of zoology. He meets a fossil fish; he cannot classify it without a knowledge of the 'Pisces.' A fossil leaf is found; a knowledge of botany is invoked, a new incentive is given to the pursuit of that study. An impression of an insect meets him; he finds that insects belong to the class ' Annulosa,' and that they are divided into families according to the structure of their wings. He pursues his inquiries into the insect world, and becomes more and more enraptured with the study of life, past and present, vegetable and animal; a new incentive is given to his, if not aimless, oftentimes fruitless walks, and he finds his mind expanding more and more in friendly rivalry with a well-exercised body, developing more and more towards physical health. Nor do his researches stop here. He comes across a piece of flint, a piece of chalk, sandstone, or limestone. It is not enough that this stone which he has just picked up is a flint; geology tells him so much. But on analysing it he finds it is pure silica or oxide of silicon? What is silicon? What is an oxide? He finds he must know something of the chemical elements silicon and oxygen; a stimulant is thus given to the study of chemistry. He, perhaps, finds a lump of galena, or sulphide of lead. It is acted on by gravity in a much greater degree than a piece of chalk or carbonate of lime would be; chalk takes a scratch more easily than galena, which, therefore, has a greater degree of hardness. Galena appears in a crystalline form; the variety of carbonate of lime called chalk is amorphous; chalk is easily decomposed by calcining, galena resists the action of heat more powerfully. To understand these differences he finds he must have an acquaintance with mineralogy and its kindred science of beautiful forms, crystallography. Thus his mind expands more and more towards a thorough appreciation of the natural sciences, not as so many dissociated branches of knowledge, but each as contributing its quota of interest to the study of Nature as a harmonious combination of varied pursuits, all pointing to a more appreciative understanding of the birth, life, and decay of the many forms of life which he sees around him; the generative forces which bring about the birth, the mysterious force of life itself, and the chemical and other forces which are called into play after the failure of the organism to sustain itself longer in the living world. So a study of one phase of nature begets an interest in another, and the geologist becomes a zoologist, a botanist, chemist, and mineralogist in turn. What a vast field is opened, therefore, to the naturalist in his country rambles! How different his gaze from that of the common sightseer as he looks around him—on the field blossoming with wild-flowers, on the sparrow's nest in the hedge, or that of the martin in the holes scooped out in the sides of the sand-pit; on the boulders which he sees on all sides, each stamped with its own particular sermon; with what interest does he not regard the huge chalk-pit cut out in the side of the Downs, where he eagerly seizes the opportunity of collecting monuments of life as it was lived æons ago!

Let us, therefore, take a naturalist's ramble across the South Downs, and, with a naturalist's eye, look intently on whatever may cross our path. We have left Brighton, and are travelling in a north-easterly direction towards Lewes, intending to traverse Stanmer Park, now the residence of the son of the late Earl of Chichester, from whom, should we have required it, we might have safely reckoned on a naturalist's interest in a naturalist's rambles. Thence we will cut across the Downs, and so out on to the Weald. With a warm sun overhead and a cool wind at our back, we soon arrive at the pretty village of Stanmer. We then find ourselves ascending the hill towards a thick wood, through which the road we are following leads, but which is soon lost in the wide expanse before us, where all is road, and no road at all. What of this wood through which we pass? It seems to contain representatives of each of the principal divisions of botanical science. We find here such flowerless plants as the ferns, mosses, and lichens;* also, the flowering plants,† viz., (1) those bearing naked or open seeds, as the fir and pine,‡ and (2) those with closed seed-vessels, as the oak, beech, etc.,§ these latter belonging to that division of plants bearing flowers, or seed-vessels, known as the Dicotyledons, or two seed-lobed plants. Each and every one of these divisions, each and every individual tree, leaf,

---

* Cryptogams.   † Phanerogams.
‡ Gymnosperms.   § Angiosperms.

fern, or flower, will furnish food for philosophy to the thoughtful rambler. To him who has a predilection for the observation of Nature, it will only serve to create a more keen appetite to master all that is known and all that can be learnt that has reference to that study. How plentifully the wild strawberry clusters amongst the undergrowth of the banks on either side of our path, shooting out its tendrils and taking fresh root, reminding one of the banyan tree, of which we have all read, but which, perhaps, very few have seen.

Before leaving the wood through which we are now passing, it might be as well to inquire why we find, scattered here and there along the range of Downs, these detached clumps of trees. We have been led to believe that the depth of earth above the chalk, never exceeding but a few inches, gave rise only to the short sweet herbage on which our Southdown flocks love to feed. To answer this we must enter somewhat into the geological history of the Downs.

The cretaceous system of strata, or that of which the chalk forms the most important subdivision, encounters us immediately preceding the Tertiary strata, and thus is of comparatively recent date in geological history. The chalk was deposited on another formation, an estuarine formation known as the Wealden. This crops out at the surface, and forms the soil between (following the Brighton main railway line) Redhill and Hassocks, *i.e.*, between the North and

South Downs. Although, now, this break occurs in the continuation of the chalk between the above-mentioned places, at one time it entirely covered the Weald.　Before, however, it underwent the enormous denudation which we know it did undergo, it is agreed by geologists that it was overlaid to a considerable depth by Tertiary formations, such as those on which London is situated, those which are visible in Hampshire and the Isle of Wight, and also those Eocene Tertiary deposits which form Furze Hill, Brighton, and Castle Hill, Newhaven.　These deposits we are led to infer at one time were continuous with one another, the chalk being entirely hidden by them. Doubtless, there must have been considerable and frequent oscillations of the level of the land in order that these Tertiaries might be deposited, that, for instance, the *marine* Thanet sands might be overlaid by the *estuarine* Woolwich series, these by the old *beaches* which formed the Oldhaven beds, and these again by the *deep-sea* deposit known as the London clay.　Although each of these must have suffered denudation in turn by the sea or estuary which deposited the succeeding strata, yet these successive denudations fall into insignificance when compared with that which took place when the chalk, and with it the Tertiaries resting on its shoulders, finally rose from beneath the waves.　Not only were the Tertiary beds in those places where we see the chalk exposed wholly swept away, but the work of destruction in-

cluded much of the chalk itself. Numerous large
rivers must have cut their way through it, denuding
the then upraised land, now known as the Weald.
Then the English Channel came to be formed, and
England was finally separated from the Continent by
the 'silver streak,' when the sea burst through the
Straits of Dover on the re-elevation of the land, at the
close of the epoch of glaciers and icebergs. Lyell, at
one time, went so far as to say that the sea itself
flowed in between the North and South Downs, and
thus formed the escarpments overlooking the Weald.
It is now generally considered that the district was
denuded almost entirely by sub-aërial agencies, by the
work of the ancient representatives of the streams now
known as the Ouse, Arun, Adur, Cuckmere, etc., and
those streams which must have excavated the many
winding valleys of the Downs. These winding valleys
are seen to branch and give out tributary valleys on
either side for miles and miles, like the windings and
tributaries of a once-existing river. What then became
of this vast amount of denuded material? We can
only judge that it went to form other deposits elsewhere, to fill up the beds of existing rivers, to form
the alluvium which skirts the southern rivers, or was
carried to the sea, where geologists of centuries to
come will meet with strata at present unknown to us.
That which concerns us, however, is the fact that
wrecks of this denudation occur in the shape of rich
patches of soil now resting, at intervals, on the chalk.

In the places where these patches occur, are found those clumps of trees which we occasionally meet with in our rambles on the Downs. They consist of the wrecks of the Eocene and chalk beds, and are generally found in hollows, or on the slopes of hills. They are composed of a rich loam with flints; occasionally lumps of ironstone, selenite,* and websterite† are found; in fact, a heterogeneous mixture of the various materials found in existing Tertiary beds. The rich loam which forms the matrix generally supports a vegetation so far out of the ordinary as to strike one's attention when on the Downs, and to this loam we owe those shady woods, so few and far between, which break the silent monotony of the South Downs.‡

We are now approaching the end of our path through the wood, and are soon out on the wide, wide Down. For the first time we take a deep breath of the beautiful, bracing air which fans our

---

* Sulphate of lime.   † Sub-sulphate of alumina.

‡ To those who are acquainted with the town of Brighton, it may be interesting to know that the Montpellier district, the Furze Hill district, and the Steine Valley, owe their vegetation to these past Tertiary deposits, known to local geologists as the Temple Field deposit, and the Coombe Rock or Elephant Bed. This deposit occurs as wedge-shaped masses eating into the chalk, and often is of serious importance in laying the foundations of buildings. Notably that of All Saints' Church tower proved a very expensive affair, and even now the tower is unfinished, and has been so for years, owing doubtless to the insecurity of the foundations.

cheeks, air untainted by smoky fog, with no one near
with whom to share it, with no trace of decaying
vegetable matter to pollute it. No; all is pure.
With buoyant heart, and still more buoyant limbs,
we skim over the elastic turf, we leave all thought of
town and business life behind us, intent on enjoying
to the utmost the health of body and wealth of knowledge which we see opened up in the path before us.
Let the Highlander talk of the rugged beauty of his
mountain home, let him praise it to the utmost as
the nurture-ground of the faithful and free, let him
sing it in his native rhyme as the birthplace and
cradle of the doer of many a doughty deed, as the
tuition ground on which was cultured that romantic
spirit of heroism and freedom which pervades the
Scot of the present day; but give me, I say, my
native Down, on whose bosom many a noble ancestor
lived and fought for his native home against the continual stream of invading hordes, whereon many a
noble and glorious fight was fought, where many a
patriotic soul bit the dust, and whereon oft invaders
and invaded met and tried their strength for the
mastery and the dominion of the British Isles. Give
me the white chalk cliffs of Albion, whose front has
borne the brunt of invasion after invasion by our ancestors of many a noble race, whose blood now flows
proudly in our veins, and from whom the English-
man has reaped those noble and high-minded qualities
which characterize him wherever on the globe we

meet him. We of the south can look back on as noble a history as the natives of any part of the British Isles, and can afford to look without envy, but rather with pride, on the noble doings of the ancestors of any of the many noble races that have peopled our country from time to time. Although we cannot offer the northerner the rugged mountain climbs and other opportunities for exercise available in his district, we can invite him to join us in breathing the pure, bracing air to be obtained in such a ramble as that we are taking.

We are now making our way along the base of a winding valley, whose turnings and meanderings suggest the only possible answer to the question as to how they were formed. Take your stand for a few minutes at the top of one of the banks at your side, or follow the valley to its fountain-head, until you are led to what may be called its watershed, and there in a moment the picture flashes before your eyes of numberless streams and rivulets, all rushing seawards, carrying in their bosom the sediments drained from hills which gave them birth, crossing and intersecting one another like a series of lakes, or meandering in most regular order like one of the mighty American rivers in miniature. Gaze on these valleys, and remember that you are looking on a picture that Nature painted by her own instruments of destruction and denudation, before man had attained even the rudiments of civilization, at a time when these calm, peaceful Downs were the scene of tumultuous rushings of waters, bearing away the accumulation of centuries seawards, at a time when the chalk rose dripping from a glacial sea and shook for ever from her shoulders the covering of ice-sheets and glaciers, under which she had for so long laboured. One might almost fancy one saw dart across the stream which filled the valley we have traversed, the long slim canoe of the drift man, as he passed from one island to another of the archipelago now being elevated above the sea. One could all but fancy one saw the picture of a new world rising from beneath a deluge of waters, icebergs, and glaciers, the connection between the previous world and the new being preserved only by a few interglacial Palæolithic men in these regions, or by the surviving species of animals in those parts unaffected by glacial conditions.

Be this fancy or be it not; the fact remains that the line of demarcation is most marked between the glacial (Pleistocene) age and the Prehistoric age. On either side of important rivers are always to be found terraces of gravel, sand, etc., cut out by the river, at different levels, and in them are found Palæolithic (Pleistocene) implements and bones of mammals, these sometimes being at a height of 100 feet, while Prehistoric remains are found only to the extent of a few feet of alluvium, etc., at the beds of, or in immediate proximity to, the rivers as they are now found. This seems to show that at some one period an enormous catastrophe by water took place, when rivers cut their present beds through previous accumulations, leaving at other levels terraces, etc., to mark their previous extent and sphere of influence. These facts seem to suggest that during the time when rivers of some magnitude were flowing in the place of our miniature rivers, they suddenly became burdened with an augmented supply of water, which necessarily increased the rapidity of · their flow, and furnished them consequently with greater power to carve out and deepen their bed. They, therefore, on the diminution of this supply of water, would continue to flow in the deeper bed that they had carved out, leaving far above them the old beaches and terraces which bounded their former banks. (At whatever time this happened, it must have been at a time sufficiently long after the glacial epoch to allow of the deposition of the gravels and river-terraces through which the rivers subsequently cut their course.)

To return to our journey. We have ascended from the valley, and can see before us Ditchling Beacon, the highest point in Sussex, and commanding a magnificent view of the Weald. We collect on our way several specimens of land shells, now mostly untenanted, and bleached white by the heat of the sun. By diligently and perseveringly examining the many flints and specimens of weathered chalk which we find scattered about, we are enabled to add various interesting specimens to our collection. Now and then, a fossil shell embedded in a flint rewards our search, or on splitting open a flint nodule we find the powdery remains of what was once a sponge, and even now we can trace its exterior form in the hollow cavity in the flint. Thus do we veritably find sermons in stones. Take in your hand a weathered flint, many specimens of which lie about your path; think over the changes it has gone through; muse over its life's history, its place of birth and mode of formation, the forces which brought its particles together in the sea which deposited the chalk, its period of inhumation beneath an ever-increasing load of accumulating strata; consider the ages, countless in our sight, which elapsed before its burden by denudation was washed away; then it was rolled and chipped about in chequered career until on the recession of the waters it was left, perhaps in the self-same spot where we find it, a silent witness to both passing political changes and to past physical revolutions. There it has lain, in all probability, since the time when Britain was united to the Continent, and, like the remains of the Neolithic Flint Implement Factory at Cissbury, has since remained untouched, save by the hand of time, through ages successively marked by Celt, Roman, Saxon, and Norman.

Such thoughts as these flash through our mind as we grasp this relic of the past. They make us attach more value to it as we handle it, they cause us to think more kindly over this aggregation of silicon and oxygen, and to perceive something worthy of thought and admiration, even in what, after all, to most people, is but a common flint.

But now we are stepping on to the Beacon, from which, and to which, was flashed, before the age of the telegraph, three centuries ago, the news which stirred the patriotism of every soul throughout the land—the news that the Invincible Armada had been sighted and was now threatening our hallowed shores. As we gain the brow of the hill, the escarpment of the Downs, we realize the effect of the war-beacon on the thousands of homesteads clustered in the plain below. We hear again the bustle and excitement of preparations for our country's defence, the clatter of horse, or the steady tramp of the men of Sussex marching to join their noble Queen at Tilbury. Macaulay's lines are called to remembrance, and we feel again those patriotic feelings which rose in our breasts when we heard the lines brilliantly rendered by an accomplished reciter. A grand scene is unfolded to our view below. Scores of villages are there, and numerous farms, surrounded each by its colony of tiny cottages, stand out amidst the hedgerowed fields like so many toy houses, each with its little garden, for so does every field appear to us from our elevated place of view.

But now our ramble is at an end. We have crossed the range of Downs, and descend into the pretty

country below. A majestically winding road of
Roman age takes us down the side of the hill, past
numerous chalk-pits, across the outcrop of the Gault
and Greensand strata, and a short walk brings us to the
little village of Ditchling. There we can turn and
look towards the hills, and realize how wisely such
commanding spots were oft selected as the camping-
ground for the invading Romans. A source of strength,
they guard our southern shore, but we can well see
how, in the hands of an enemy, they might indeed
become a source of weakness.

CHAPTER XI.

A GEOLOGICAL JOURNEY FROM LONDON TO BRIGHTON.

'As firm as the mountains'—World-making—Geological Systems —The subsoils of London—Purley chalk-pit—North Downs —Billiard-table of Sussex—The Weald—The great Iguanodon —Pouched animals in England—Elephant bed—Strange fossils at Brighton.

I T is surprising that so little interest is felt by the majority of people as to the nature of the ground over which they tread, whether, for instance, it is composed of sand, or clay, or limestome, and whether the strata which form the various soils and subsoils were laid down by the sea or by the agency of rivers. Many have still no other thought than that the land always existed in the same condition as that in which we now see it, and that where now are mountains, valleys, and forests, there was never aught else to be found, some, perhaps, still entertaining the belief that no alteration in the configuration of the land masses has taken place since the earth's creation. This is undoubtedly erroneous, and it will be necessary at once to state that our present continents are merely in a state of transition, and that the phrase 'as firm as the mountains' has, geologically speaking, no force whatever. The elevation of most of the stupendous ranges of mountains existing on the earth's surface took place at a comparatively recent date, although some of the lesser ranges belong to a considerably older period. Amongst the best known of these are the low ranges of hills familiar to us as the North and South Downs, which were formed at the latter end of what is known as the Secondary epoch, although, of course, they have since been raised to their present elevation. They will occupy a share of our attention on our journey to Brighton.

Beneath our feet there exist layer upon layer of sedimentary material, which have been piled upon the top of each other to a depth of not less perhaps than twelve miles. They have not been deposited continuously. Between many of the layers there exists a visible break, shown in some cases by the brecciated nature of the material at the junction of the formations. This break in the deposition of the strata would occur when an area, which had been submerged, again became dry land, other layers afterwards being thrown upon it when the sea or other body of water again covered it. The fossil forms in these two sets of strata would differ according as the interval of time between each successive deposit was long or short. To mention one case, the chalk strata are seen at Charlton with the Thanet Sands reposing upon them, and at the junction of the two the chalk is seen to have suffered great aqueous erosion. Some ten or twelve inches of débris, consisting principally of rolled flints, which have been washed out and rounded by the action of the sea, are found resting upon the chalk, although beneath the Tertiaries. The fossil remains of the chalk differ entirely from those of the Eocene (to which the Thanet Sands belong), certain forms of life having during the interval become extinct, and given place to those which are peculiar to the Eocene age.

The strata, or layers, to which I have referred, have been arranged by geologists, according to the mineralogical and palæontological characters with which they are stamped, into twelve grand systems, beneath which occurs what is supposed to be the original surface of the earth, denuded, of course, by miles of material which might have been worn down in intermediate ages to form the various strata which now rest upon it.

Between London and Brighton none of the Primary or Palæozoic rocks come to the surface. During our journey, we shall be principally concerned with the more recent portion of the Secondary age, as well as some of the succeeding Tertiaries. The following table will illustrate the formations with which we shall be concerned :—

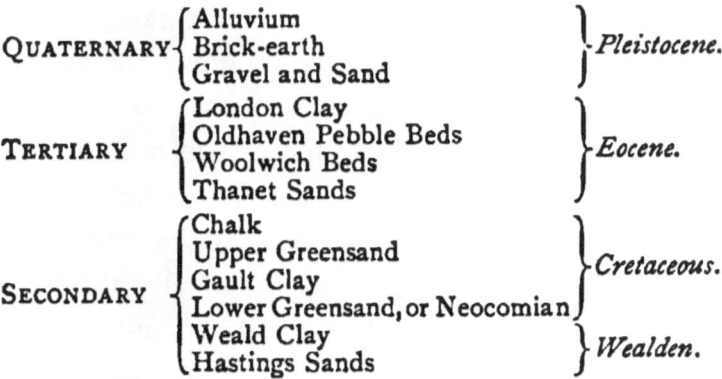

QUATERNARY	Alluvium Brick-earth Gravel and Sand	Pleistocene.
TERTIARY	London Clay Oldhaven Pebble Beds Woolwich Beds Thanet Sands	Eocene.
SECONDARY	Chalk Upper Greensand Gault Clay Lower Greensand, or Neocomian	Cretaceous.
	Weald Clay Hastings Sands	Wealden.

I propose to examine the nature of the strata in question, by taking one of the slow trains of the Brighton Railway Company, and examining the banks and cuttings on both sides as we travel southwards.

Starting from London Bridge, the most recent deposit, the *Alluvium*, occupies the whole of Bermondsey on the north-east of the railway, and also the Isle of Dogs and the Greenwich Marshes, but dwindles to an insignificant patch by the side of the river westward. London Bridge terminus and Waterloo are situated upon it. It would seem that our ancestors, when they first decided to adopt the site of London as the position for their future city, marched up the river until they had left the alluvium behind, doubtless being fully aware of the undesirability of building on this low-lying impervious soil. In the east of London, especially on the north side of the river, it occupies broad tracts, although in the west it is only found along the immediate banks of the Thames.

The deposit of *Brick-earth* is an extremely local one, and occurs in the vicinity of New Cross and Peckham. Mr. Whitaker says, 'This loam, or mixture of clay and sand, is more local than the gravel on which it rests, though it nevertheless takes up some space. It is of brown colour and of no great thickness, and, being more or less clayey, tends to prevent water from sinking to the gravel.' It is so called in consequence of its constituents forming good material for the making of bricks. This quality was taken advantage of, I am told, at a place known as Red Hill, in Greenwich, where to stay the denuding action of the atmosphere upon it, the hill was burnt, so to speak, forming it into a hard rock-like substance.

The next formation, the *gravel and sand*, occupies a good deal of space in South London, and together with the Brick-earth constitutes the Valley or River Drift, having been deposited at times when the Thames was a much wider river than now, or perhaps when it left its burden of sediment after periodical floods. A soil composed of this mixture of sand and gravel is, I need scarcely say, a healthy one on which to live, owing to the sand giving passage for the drainage of superfluous water. It supplies all the shallow wells, and extends sometimes to a depth of twenty feet.

But now we have passed over the ground occupied by the Quaternary deposits, and are travelling over the outcrop of the Woolwich Beds, which we have described elsewhere in treating of the London Basin, and which we soon leave behind as we pass Brockley Station. The London Clay next demands our attention, and occupies the ground beneath us as we travel through the suburban stations between Brockley and Croydon.* Immediately after passing Croydon, a cutting may be seen on our right, some two hundred yards away, where the Thanet Sands, the lowest member of the Tertiary strata, are to be seen. The sections are known in the neighbourhood as the ballast-pits. These beds are the last to crop out before encountering the chalk, and have at their base a layer which is impervious to water, so that many wells in South London are supplied from this source.

Having journeyed over the extreme limits of what is known as the London Basin, the chalk strata, the uppermost layer of the Cretaceous system, gradually rises from beneath our feet. If we watch the sides of the cuttings through which we pass, we at once recognise the white amorphous form of carbonate of lime known as chalk. We notice a large chalk-pit at Purley Station, where a great portion of the hill has been carried away for the manufacture of lime. By means of calcining, the chalk is split up into lime and carbonic acid, the suffocating effect produced by the latter being at once evident in the vicinity of the lime-kilns. The railway as far as Merstham has been

* See page 95.

laid down in a cutting in the rock, and when we pass through Merstham Tunnel we are travelling under the highest part of the range of hills known as the North or Surrey Downs.

It is interesting to note that roads and railways almost invariably lie in close proximity to one another, and that they usually follow the direction of some of the many river-valleys which intersect a chalky country. In these valleys are often found beds of flints, which at once bespeak the source whence they have been derived, viz., from the chalk itself. The conclusion arrived at is that these hills must have been intersected in Tertiary ages by numerous rivers and streams, at the time, perhaps, that the chalk was elevated from the Cretaceous sea, when an enormous amount of denudation took place as the waves gradually receded from it. The rivers would bear away the light particles of the chalk, but the heavy flints would sink to the bottom, remaining where they were thus deposited as evidence to us in the present age of the amount of denudation which had taken place. It is in consequence of such beds of flint occurring in different parts of Surrey and Sussex, where the chalk is not now to be found, that we judge and decide that at a period remote from now the chalk entirely covered the Weald.

We have now emerged from Merstham Tunnel, and the least observant person can at once see that a great change comes over the scene. Instead of seeing the rounded heights of the Downs encircling us on every side, we are leaving the hills far away behind, and are gliding smoothly over a wide area of flat tableland, which we shall continue to notice until we arrive at Three Bridges. Immediately on leaving the tunnel we pass over the outcrops from beneath the chalk of the Upper Greensand, the Gault, and, as we approach Redhill, the Lower Greensand. Here the latter formation rises to a considerable altitude, and instead of being green, as its name would imply, presents a reddish appearance. This is shown in the cutting on our left, through which the South-Eastern Railway branches off to Tunbridge Wells, and in the pits of sand which can be seen on our right, just after passing the railway-station.

We soon, however, leave the Lower Greensand behind, and at Earlswood pass on to the Weald clay, which, with the Hastings Sands over which we travel at Three Bridges, go to make up the Wealden formation. The country occupied by this series of strata has a very regular and smooth surface, and is known in some parts as the 'Billiard-table of Sussex.'

The Hastings Sands are so called from the town of Hastings, which is situated on a continuation of the beds eastward. The whole Wealden formation, therefore, covers almost the entire area between the North and South Downs, and presents such an appearance as would be caused by the wasting away of material between the two ranges and the laying bare of the older formation beneath. The North Downs, roughly speaking, have their termination eastward at the Fore-land, whilst the South Downs end abruptly at Beachy Head. The Weald clay and Hastings Sands approach the sea and form the coast line between the two pro-montories, so that if we were to prepare a diagram showing a section of the strata around the coast of Kent and Sussex, it would be very similar indeed to one prepared to show a section between the North and South Downs. It is thus, then, that we find Hastings situated on the sands of that name, on the coast between the two points mentioned.

We have now passed Three Bridges, and we begin to notice a change in the aspect of the country. In-stead of a flat table-land of clay, we notice that the new formation is thrown up in a very irregular manner, constituting what are known as the Wealden Heights. We observe the strata at the side of the various railway cuttings as we pass through them, and perceive that they dip northward at an angle of about 25°, some-times more and sometimes less, as if at some point at which we have not yet arrived the strata have been subjected to a great upheaval. This we shall find has been the case in the vicinity of Balcombe, where the highest parts of the range occur, and whence the strata, bending over, dip in an opposite direction, and form somewhere about this point what is known as a 'saddle-back,' or a 'Forest Ridge,' as it is called. A great part of it has subsequently been removed by denudation. Here we pass through Bal-

combe Tunnel, and perhaps if our journey has here-
tofore taken place on a rainy day, we shall emerge
under quite a different sky, for it has often been
noticed that the hills represented to us by the tunnel
are sufficient to be the cause of a distinct change of
atmospheric conditions, which we may notice in passing from one side to the other. We notice, too,
that several of the bridges under which we pass are
built of material quarried from the local sandstone
formation. In Kent extensive use is made of this
stone for building purposes, the churches of Staple-
hurst, Cranbrook, Goudhurst, Hawkhurst, and others,
being built almost entirely of it.

On the right of the railway as we pass through
Balcombe Tunnel is the woodland district known as
Tilgate Forest, in whose quarries Dr. Mantell pursued
his studies concerning the Wealden formation, and in
which he found the fossil remains of the great land-
reptile *Iguanodon Mantelli*, and to which he gave his
name. This animal, which rivalled the elephant in
size, had two long hind-legs and two short front ones,
supporting itself like the modern kangaroo. From the
appearance presented by its teeth having been ground
down, it has been judged that it was a vegetarian
feeder. One specimen which has been put together
in the Brussels Museum proves it to have been more
than thirty feet in height.

A number of lower jaws of small marsupials or
pouched mammals have been found in what are known

as the Purbeck Beds and the Stonesfield Slate, divisions of the Oolitic system which are not very far removed, geologically, from the Wealden formation.　Thus the period brings to our notice a state of affairs existent in these regions, similar to that now found among the animal kingdom in Australia.　This is the principal part of the world where pouched animals are now found. Geology shows us that at the time we are considering they existed in these northern regions; but have in the course of time given way to a fauna more highly organized and more able to withstand the vicissitudes of our climate.

We have now passed over the following formations :—

> Quaternary,
> Tertiary (Eocene),
> Cretaceous,
> Wealden,

and, having crossed the saddleback ridge of the Weald, we shall again encounter the same series of strata, only that this time they will be in the reverse order, and will dip away in an opposite direction, namely, to the south.

On arriving at Keymer Junction station we again meet the Weald Clay which we lost at Three Bridges, and at the next station, Burgess Hill, we once more pass on to the Cretaceous formation.　We shortly after enter the tunnel at Clayton, which is pierced through the chalk of the South Downs.　We soon

6

arrive at Brighton Station and pass through another Quaternary accumulation known as the Elephant Bed, or Coombe Rock.

The two great systems which we have just traversed, the Wealden and the Cretaceous, differ from one another in this most fundamental principle, that whereas the chalk is a deep-sea deposit, containing a truly marine fauna, the Wealden is either freshwater or brackish, and therefore contains fossils peculiar to those formations. Earlier geologists could not understand how such a vast estuary deposit as the Weald could possibly have been overlaid by the chalk to a depth of some 1,000 feet. It would have necessitated adopting the belief that the earth's surface must have receded below the waves, and have been subsequently re-elevated into dry land. This, however, is the belief which has since been adopted, and indeed without any very great stretch of the imagination, since many other instances have been encountered in geological history, of submergence and re-elevation in the same place, perhaps two or three times repeated.

The chalk is almost entirely composed of the microscopic calcareous and silicious coverings of myriads of minute Foraminifera. Much light has been thrown on the formation of chalk by discoveries made by the *Challenger* expedition, when on examination of ooze brought up from the bottom of the Atlantic during the deep-sea dredging, it was found to consist principally of foraminiferal shells of various genera, the *Globigerina*, the same genus that is found in the chalk, predominating. The silicious shells of Polycystinæ, and the silicious skeletons of microscopic plants called Diatomaciæ, were found, together with the silicious spicules of sponges. It may readily be conceived that the silica for producing the flints which intersect the chalk in vertical and horizontal bands may have had its origin in these innumerable silicious bodies.

The Wealden, on the other hand, is a freshwater deposit, assuming in some parts an estuarine character. Travelling west to east, we find that its fossil remains become more and more allied to those known to inhabit brackish waters. It is argued from this, and on other grounds, that the strata were deposited in the bed of a ·gigantic river flowing towards the east from far out in the Atlantic, and entering the North Sea of those days. This formation is not only developed in southern England, but in the Netherlands, the interval forming at this period a large estuary to a mighty river, draining the raised bed of the Atlantic, and rivalling in size the great American rivers.

Ironstone occurs in such abundance and purity in the Weald that, previous to the development of the iron-smelting trade in the north, it was largely quarried for economic purposes. It is interesting to note that the railing which encloses St. Paul's Cathedral is made from iron worked in the Weald. Blocks of ironstone may be seen by the side of the railway north of Haywards Heath station, where for some distance the strata have been laid bare by the widening of the cutting to allow room for the new line of rails to East Grinstead.

We have now arrived within sight of our destination, and observe that the Brighton terminus has been cut out of the side of a chalk hill. When the site was excavated it was found necessary to cut through a Quaternary formation on the chalk known as the 'Elephant Bed,' so called because bones of that animal had been found in the bed as exhibited elsewhere. This excavation created great interest in the geological world, all manner of bones and carved flints, etc., being found there; bones which, when examined, were found to belong to animals of very recent date, such as the common ox, sheep, etc. In fact, one individual was caught depositing these 'fossils' in the bed one night, for enthusiastic palæontologists to discover the next day, and dilate upon in their works to an interested and wonder-stricken world!

We have now traversed, geologically, the line between London and Brighton, and maybe these pages will cause him who reads them to take an interest in the country when gliding towards the Queen of Watering-places. It is a journey which is being travelled yearly by many thousands of people,

and the *ennui* often begotten by an hour in the
railway train may perhaps be provided against by
evincing an interest, although slight and perhaps
passing, in the geology of the district travelled
through.

CHAPTER XII.

A TALE OF TWO TEETH.

An ancient world—An ancient occupant—A very useful tooth—
A sufferer from toothache.

I HAVE a tooth which measures eight inches in length, six inches in depth, and three inches across the crown. I have another measuring an eighth of an inch in length, depth, and thickness. No, dear reader, neither of them at any time belonged to a human creature; they have come into my possession as relics of those that lived in an age long anterior to that in which you and I live.

Both these teeth have a characteristic story of their own to tell.

The first, the larger of the two, stood originally in the mouth of an animal belonging to the elephant tribe, *elephas primigenius*, more familiarly known as the mammoth.

On the coast of Norfolk and Suffolk, the relics of a formation are to be found, which extends in some

parts beneath the sea, and which, in the neighbourhood of Cromer, is known as the Cromer Forest Bed.
There are other forest beds to be found around the
coast of Britain, all of which were overwhelmed by the
sea in prehistoric times, when the ocean gradually en-
croached on the land, and washed large quantities of
its débris into the area of the primæval forest which
had till then existed. The trees became rooted up
by the violence of the sea, and buried in the bed of
the advancing ocean, and a proof of this is to be found
in the fact that stumps and trunks of trees are even
now being thrown up on the coasts of our eastern
counties.

In the forest there had roamed many of the
large mammals which characterised tertiary ages, and
amongst them was this extinct elephant. The owner
of this particular tooth may have died before his
forest home met with its final annihilation, or he
may have been a solitary survivor of his species, who
lived to see the wreck of the forest in which he and
his comrades had disported themselves. Any way,
when at last he shuffled off his mortal coil, his bones
found a grave beneath the ocean, and there were
rolled and tossed about by tide and current until one
by one they became disjointed, and scattered about in
the bed of the sea.

The teeth of this animal possessed a very useful
quality, which cannot but cause a pang of regret to
many who read of it, that the same benefit was not

extended to those of the human species. This was a continual growing of tooth material, from the back to the front of the mouth, so that as by continual grinding the tooth was worn away, a fresh growth replaced that which was lost. The crown of the tooth, as we look upon it, is seen to consist of ten parallel folds of enamel, the foremost five being in a perfected condition, whilst the five posterior folds have not yet attained their full development.

This tooth, too, served a useful purpose, even when seemingly lost to all knowledge at the bottom of the ocean. It became the dwelling-place of various minute marine animals, which made use of it in the same way as those which we see covering a scallop-shell when fresh from the sea. In some parts it became enveloped by one of the little compound animals, the *Flustra* or sea-mat, consisting of a number of organisms similar in external structure to the coral polype, united to one another to form one common polyzoarium; in others by a white chalky layer of acorn shells or *Balani*, similar to those which encrust the piles of piers between high and low water-mark.

After a long period of submarine existence, it was dredged up by some Lowestoft fishermen, and brought ashore with its covering organisms complete. It then passed into my possession, and has since proved a very useful and interesting geological specimen.

Many useful ornaments are made of these fossil

teeth, since they are composed of good ivory, and are susceptible of a fine smooth polish.

The second tooth mentioned above does not, perhaps, possess such an important history.

It is one of a series of small teeth which were extracted from the chalk cliff near Rottingdean, on the Sussex coast.

A violent storm was just subsiding with the ebbing tide. The fury of the waves as they lashed the foot of the cliffs when the storm was at it highest had worn away the chalk around that part where these teeth were imbedded. Being, however, of a harder texture than the surrounding chalk, they had resisted for a time the action of the waves, and the tide had receded, leaving them abutting from the chalky matrix. As the largest of them was not so much as a half an inch in length, however, it required close observation in order to detect them, and a search resulted in the discovery of others of a smaller size. Their proximity to one another in the cliff would seem to point to their having belonged at some period to one and the same animal—in this case a fish of the shark tribe.

One of the larger of them was peculiarly worn away, and in such a manner that it seemed to suggest that it had been subject to a decay such as even we human owners of teeth experience. Whether the decaying process commenced in this tooth while as yet its owner lived, or whether the decay was of more recent origin, we can but speculate. We have heard that the monkey at the Zoological Gardens lost his toothache when a decaying molar was extracted, but whether a fish ever suffered from the malady is a question for discussion. We will charitably hope that decay of the teeth is not of such ancient origin as the chalk period, and that this tooth in particular was not the cause of suffering to its fishy owner.

CHAPTER XIII.

THE GEOLOGICAL POSITION OF LONDON.

The London Basin—Sections at the Charlton pits—A shell-marble—Pebble-beds—The London Clay—From a tropical to an arctic climate—Ice-sheets and glaciers.

IF a Londoner were to bore immediately beneath his feet he would find that he must pierce through some hundreds of feet of clay and sand before arriving at the well-known chalk beds, which he sees out-cropping at the surface of the land both north and south of London and its suburbs. As he travelled southward from the Thames towards the Downs he would find the chalk at a gradually decreasing depth, and as he went northward from the same line of division he would meet with a similar experience.

This is because the chalk is at its greatest depth in the valley of the Thames, and either north or south from it the bed gradually rises towards the surface.

The shape of the chalk strata resembles, therefore, that of a trough or basin, and in this the various tertiary beds have been deposited which occur in what is known as the LONDON BASIN.

But in London proper, with the exception of a small district at Lewisham and Charlton, the chalk does not appear at the surface at all, being regularly covered by one or more formations belonging to the Eocene age. The chalk as it approaches London from the south most aggravatingly sinks beneath the surface at an imaginary line joining the towns of Epsom, Sutton, Croydon, Orpington, and Seven Oaks, and to such a depth that at the spot where a shaft was sunk by the Southwark and Vauxhall Water Company at Streatham a year or two ago, the chalk was only arrived at after traversing 900 feet of tertiary beds of clay, gravel, and sand. When, however, we pass beyond the northernmost limits of London, we again find the chalk immediately beneath our feet, cropping out from beneath these tertiary beds at a line joining the towns of Watford, Rickmansworth, Beaconsfield, Marlow, Maidenhead, on to Reading and Hungerford, and forming the long southern slopes of the Chiltern Hills.

Thus we see that the whole of the Metropolis and the beds on which it is built are held in a trough of the chalk, the hills forming a natural boundary both north and south. The beds above the chalk may be classified as follows :—

1. { Made earth (in central London).
   { Alluvium.

2. { Brick Earth.
      Gravel and Sand.
3. Boulder Clay (Glacial).
4. London Clay.
5. Oldhaven (pebble) Beds.
6. Woolwich and Reading Beds.
7. Thanet Sands.

A few characteristics of each of these, and the places where they can be seen, may be of interest to the casual geologist.

The Thanet Sands (7) are one of the most well-marked divisions of the tertiary strata. They attain their greatest thickness on the north-east coast of Kent, being 100 feet thick in the Isle of Thanet, and taking their name therefrom. As we approach London in a westerly direction the bed gradually thins out, so that when we reach the Bank of England it is only 40 feet thick, and at Ealing, to the west of London, it has but a thickness of eight feet. The materials of which the bed is composed have a special characteristic attaching to them, and one which serves to show to some extent the source whence the sand was derived before being laid down by the sea which once covered them. Under a microscope the particles of sand are ascertained to be of a regular crystalline form, altogether unlike the rounded grains of which sand is ordinarily composed. Now in Belgium there is a wide extent of country, the surface of which is composed of primary crystalline rocks, containing a large proportion of quartz, which as you know is exactly the same as sand and flint in its chemical composition. This fact, together with the knowledge stated above that the sands are thickest in the east and thin out to the west, serves to show that the sea denuded the crystalline rocks and washed the quartz westward, laying it down where we now see it, but only transporting the material in diminishing quantities to any distance in the west, and having no influence beyond Richmond, where it dies out. There are some sand pits at Charlton, near Woolwich, where it has a thickness of about 50 feet. Large quantities are here quarried and shipped as ballast by vessels leaving the Thames. The vertical cliff caused by these quarrying operations shows us a layer of chalk at its base, whilst between the chalk and the Thanet Sands is a thin layer, perhaps a foot thick, of flints. This layer derives its origin from the denudation of the soft chalk, the heavier flints having been left behind by the water which denuded it.

At Charlton the beds known as the Woolwich series (6) are also well developed. Similarly they are to be seen in full force at Castle Cliff, Newhaven, and at Seaford. The most remarkable feature about these beds is that they include layer after layer of shells, principally *cyrenæ*, packed tightly together in a matrix of clay. When a mass of it is dried, it bears a resemblance to the shell-marble found in the Weald, and known as Sussex or Petworth Marble. Much of the shell-sand used largely in London for spreading over garden paths is obtained from these beds.

The Oldhaven Beds (5) next to be mentioned are recognisable at once in the neighbourhood of London. In a matrix of clayey sand are contained large quantities of rounded pebbles not larger than a hen's egg, and generally smaller. These pebbles are noticed in large numbers in Greenwich Park. Blackheath itself sometimes gives its name to the series, whilst those who have visited Croham Hurst, a short distance south of Croydon, cannot but have noticed the quantity of pebbles which are trodden under foot.

All these formations, however, sink into insignificance beside the deposit of London Clay (4) which now came to be laid down. In some places it shows a thickness of as much as 500 feet. In the London Basin it covers a great part of the surface, and it is also to be found in full force in Hampshire, extending into the Isle of Wight. Looking at a geological map of the country, one cannot help being struck by a conviction that these deposits were once continuous with each other, and that the whole of the clay between Hampshire and the Thames has since been so completely washed away that now not a trace is to be found in the country between those parts.

The character of the fossils which the London clay affords, at once points it out to have been deposited in a sea perhaps quite as deep as that which in a previous age had laid down the chalk. Most of the low hills around London are formed of this clay, such as Shooter's Hill, the Sydenham Hills, Primrose Hill, etc. It consists of a stiff clay, and is always more or less damp at its surface, although the effects of this are greatly modified in a large part of South London and in the City, owing to a subsequent deposition of gravel upon it.

After the London Clay had been gradually accumulating for many ages beneath the ocean, the bed of the sea came to be gradually upheaved, until at last it appeared as dry land, the greater part of what are now the British Isles probably partaking in the upheaval. Thus during the Miocene age, which followed, no deposits were laid down in the neighbourhood of London, although during the succeeding Pliocene age the coast line again approached sufficiently near, by a submergence of the land, to allow of the deposition by the sea of those beds known on the Norfolk and Suffolk coasts as the Coralline and Red Crags.

A gradual declension of climatal temperature had been going on since the tropical times of the London Clay, through the sub-tropical Miocene age and the temperate Pliocene era, until now, at the ushering in of Pleistocene times, the climate was not far short of arctic, and indeed the country, as it then was, soon became covered by an extensive ice-sheet, and glaciers came sliding down from the higher grounds, bringing with them the products of their place of origin, and depositing their burdens as they melted in places far removed from the land of their birth. In the north of England the result has been that thick banks of clay known as 'boulder clay' and 'till' have been formed, whilst imbedded therein have been found a few species of shells of a distinctly arctic character and such as are not now found on the English coasts at all. In the north of London, on the hills of Hampstead and Highgate, a capping of this boulder clay is to be found, the valley of the Thames being a rough boundary of the southernmost sphere of the influence of glacial conditions.

But now the glacial epoch passed away, and with the melting of the ice-sheets the land became again raised above the level of the sea. The Thames and other rivers, charged with an increased volume of water over and above that which they possesséd before all were hidden beneath the sea, cut their way through the beds which surrounded them, as for instance in the case of the Thames, through the Eocene formations before mentioned—and deriving large quantities of flints from the existing Eocene pebble-beds, it proceeded to scatter them along its banks, and to deposit them in the then lower reaches of the river, thus giving rise to those wide tracts of 'Gravel and sand' (2) which cover so large an area in South London. These gravel deposits must not be confounded with certain gravel beaches and terraces which occur in the north of London, and which owe their origin to the glacial conditions already referred to as also giving rise to the boulder clays.

In approaching London from the east, as soon as we get clear of a line drawn from Greenwich through Lewisham and extended southward, we leave all the outcrops of the London Tertiaries behind, with the exception of one—viz., the London clay. This important formation, together with, in some parts, the river gravels, constitutes almost the whole of South London between the imaginary line we have drawn and a western boundary which we may fix as far west as Kingston and Wimbledon. The eastern part of Wimbledon Common is London clay, and on the west the gravels are in full force. Tooting Common is situated on the clay. North Brixton and Clapham are mostly built upon gravel, although in the latter place the clay shows itself largely in Clapham Park. Sydenham, the Crystal Palace and Forest Hill are built upon clay, but both north and south of the Palace there are two patches of gravel on the summit of the hills. Think of the time when the river was sufficiently broad to deposit this gravel, about six miles from the present river! Continuing eastward we find a thick bed of gravel following the valley of the river Ravensbourne, identical in direction with the Lewisham Road and reaching to the south of Bromley.

North of these places, and between them and the river, the surface consists of 'gravel and sand,' except, of course, in the immediate vicinity of the river. This would seem to show that the river, previously to laying down the gravel, destroyed great part of the Tertiaries, leaving only a part of the London clay exposed, and then with the denuded fragments deposited the pebbles in the form of gravel. Thus the work of destruction and denudation went on side by side with that of construction, the two actions to some extent counterbalancing one another.

It is a striking fact that the next formation—that of the alluvium (1) although found to so great an extent below London Bridge, is scarcely found at all above the bridge, and this is, indeed, very likely to have been the cause of the site on which the city was built. Over a large part of Bermondsey there appears this thick bed of river mud, while in the bed of the river eastward from London Bridge an important fault appears to have occurred, so that the strata on the north of the river have sunk down to a lower level than those on the south. The result of this fault was that the river spread itself over a wide tract of land on the north, and in prehistoric times deposited alluvium wherever it went. Even now the level is considerably lower than that on the south, and consists principally of wide stretches of marsh land.

CHAPTER XIV.

NATURAL SCIENCE JOTTINGS FROM FELIXSTOWE.

At the seaside—The Norfolk and Suffolk cliffs—Red Crag—
London Clay—Cement stones—A reversed whelk—River
Deben—Springs and streams—Miniature Cañons.

I F one were to interrogate every seaside visitor as to
the reason why, when each summer gradually
steals round, he wends his way to the wave-washed
coast, and were to ask him why he is not content to
remain amidst the surroundings of our beautiful
Metropolis, his answer would in all probability be that
he is anxious to obtain a change of air and scenery,
and throwing aside the restraints of business, to seek
above all things—rest. He thus repairs to the sea
coast, and enters with spirit into the enjoyments
which the place affords, until suddenly he awakes to a
feeling of uneasiness, and asks himself, ' What shall I
do next ?'

If anyone who reads these lines happens to light
upon the pretty little town of Felixstowe, and finds the

time hang heavily on his hands, I would ask him to make an effort towards obtaining additional pleasure from his visit by paying a little attention to what is called the natural science of the place, and to note down any points of interest which he may glean during his visit.

A glance at a map would show that Harwich is situated nearly at the mouth of the estuary of the Orwell, whilst opposite to that town a low-lying promontory stands out from the left bank of the river, and runs out to sea, with Felixstowe Railway Pier and the Fort at its termination. The promontory is about two miles and a half long, and takes its start from an old line of sea cliffs, which have been denuded by the river and the sea to form the long stretch of low ground of which the point consists. Continuing a short distance northward, the line of cliffs approaches the sea, and here, both above and below the cliffs, the town of Felixstowe stands. It was noticeable that, whereas on our south coasts the beach, being washed up the English Channel from the Atlantic, accumulated on the west sides of the groynes, on this part of the east coast the source of beach was from the north, and the groynes, such as they were, became filled on their northern side, whilst that on the south remained empty. When, therefore, the promontory in question commenced to be formed, in Pleistocene times, by the accumulation of mud brought down by the river Orwell, it received great assistance in its formation by what would appear to be in this part the prevailing southerly current. The deposit of river mud, trending in a south-easterly direction, received the full force of the sea current on its northern face, and here wide banks of sand and shingle accumulated, extending its area and receiving the denuded fragments of the cliffs to the north.

The Norfolk and Suffolk cliffs are most interesting from a geological point of view. A series of formations extends for some distance inland, now well known as the 'Crag,' which mark, by the littoral character of their deposition, the limit of the ocean which existed in Pliocene times. From Cromer, in the north, to Clacton-on-Sea, in Essex, we find, in the sea-cliffs, a succession of deposits which illustrate very forcibly both by their composition and by the fossil remains imbedded in them, the slow change which gradually came over the climate of the country. At Clacton the greater part of the cliffs consists of London clay, an extension of that bed northward which underlies the whole of London, but which, in Suffolk, becomes overlaid by the crag formations. The general inclination of the beds is at an angle of thirty-five degrees to the north, so that as we recede from London along the coast we find the older beds sinking beneath our feet, whilst those of more recent date occupy their place ; by means of the character of their fossils we are thus able to trace the gradual declension of climate which took place, which finally culminated in the glacial Pleistocene epoch to which we have before referred.

At Felixstowe the cliffs behind the houses are composed, for the most part, of ' red crag,' whilst the stiff blue London clay appears beneath and forms their basement. The line of junction is very marked, and oftentimes includes a layer of water-worn London clay ' cement-stones,' amongst which frequently occur the remains of the mastodon and other large mammals.

The London clay is familiar to all, but the Red Crag may not be so well known. The rusty colour which characterises its sand, and which has stained all the included shells red, causes its fossils to be easily recognised when seen in a museum, and has given to it the name which it bears. The fossil-hunter could never be more sure of success in his searches than when entering a red crag pit. Some parts of the cliff, in the very midst of Felixstowe, are literally packed with fossils, although, unfortunately, owing to their brittleness, many are in a broken condition. Many perfect specimens can, however, be obtained, and amongst them will at once be noticed the reversed whelk, *Fusus contrarius,* so called from its whorls being in a contrary direction to that characterising the whelk of the present day. In some places occur bands of iron-stone, where the oxide of iron, to which the whole formation is indebted for its redness, has appeared in more than ordinary strength. A characteristic fossil is the earbone of the whale, whilst the teeth of sharks occur in great abundance in some parts.

The beach in front of the town is well worth examining. Some people are said to have discovered carnelians and other rare stones. This is quite possible—agates, jasper, carnelian, chrysophrase, etc., being but different forms of silica, or as we better know it—flint. I have found sharks' teeth washed up by the sea, and also portions of fossils imbedded in flint. The rocks north of the town consist of large blocks of London clay which are covered at high tide by the sea. Shells, starfish, and wood, can be seen imbedded therein, whilst the veins of spar which permeate the masses, and which cause the nodules to become known as 'snake-stones,' are seen very clearly in these rocks at low tide. The collector, too, will be able to add something to his museum by searching among the rocks for pieces of fossil wood, petrified into iron-pyrites, and exhibiting when broken the brassy appearance common to that mineral.

At one time the London clay which forms the bed of the sea was the repository of large quantities of cement-stones which were washed out of the clay, but the dredging which was carried on for years made so great an inroad into what was once a natural break-water, that now the landowners to the north of Felixstowe are put to great pains and expense to erect artificial breakwaters, to prevent the encroachments of the sea. The fossil contents of both the most northerly and the most southerly portions of the red crag have been carefully compared, and it has been found that, whereas the shells contained in those portions which rest immediately on the London clay exhibit the characters of shells inhabiting a warm climate, those found farther north begin to differ so far from them, that it has been concluded that the latter part of the crag was deposited long after the former, and that the climate had so far cooled as not to permit of certain shells living which had existed when the formation commenced to be laid down. This was borne out by the fact that shells of a more Arctic character made their appearance in the north which are not to be found in the south. The discovery, therefore, went to support the theory of the gradual declension of the climate which went on in these times.

Felixstowe is situated on a peninsula, having the river Orwell for its southern boundary, whilst on the north it is bounded by the river Deben. This is not a very well-known river, and it is scarcely used at all for navigation, although, at its mouth, it is as wide as the Thames at London Bridge. The result has been that it has become silted up in great part, and sandbanks have accumulated around the submerged forest which existed a short distance from the coast. The banks are laid bare at low tide, and have the appearance of a number of islands. On the opposite side of the river is a large red-brick mansion, built by

Mr. Cuthbert Quilter, M.P. The river offers first-rate fishing to the angler, whilst for sailing it equals many of the Broads. On the south side are the famous Bawdsley Golf Links, about four miles from Felixstowe. An island at the mouth of the river presented, at the time I saw it, a remarkable resemblance to one of the coral islands of the Pacific of which one often reads. A circular fringe of sand-rock appeared to have been formed, perhaps assisted in its induration by the red oxide of iron washed from the cliffs with the sand of the crag, whilst inside the circle was a lagoon of smooth water, noticeable in contrast to the breakers beating upon the outer edge.

On walking along the coast to the Deben, I could not help noticing the number of springs issuing from the cliffs, but which soon became lost in the beach and sand. The rain, in sinking through the Red Crag material, of which the upper part of the cliffs was formed, was arrested when it arrived at the base of London clay; this, being impervious to water, gave rise to the springs, which issued from the cliffs where the junction of the two formations occurred. One of these springs struck me as being very interesting. It was evidently an old-established one, for it had in the course of time formed a miniature delta of its own. Just as the larger rivers have formed extensive deltas at their mouths, so this spring had brought down with it mud and sand, until it had accumulated sufficient at its point of contact with the beach to prevent it at once from sinking out of sight. This process of depositing sedimentary material had gone on until an area of mud, about twelve feet long by four broad, had become strewn out over the beach, and the point where the spring at last disappeared was some considerable distance from the cliff where it first took its rise.

This occurred to me to be exactly the same process on a small scale which is going on at the mouths of rivers —the Mississippi, for instance—where every century wide tracts of land are being formed at its mouth by the deposition of sedimentary material brought down from the higher ground. Nor was this the sole resemblance. The stream itself now only occupied a central direction through the mud, and at the sides the sediment had dried, only to be overflowed in times of flood, similar to the rise which takes place in connection with the Nile, and which is so anxiously looked forward to by the fellaheen on account of the fertile sediment it leaves behind it.

Although not personally familiar with the cañons of Colorado and Mexico, we have doubtless all read of the precipitous chasms with which the traveller there meets, of the magnificent waterfalls and cascades which leap down some hundreds of feet into the narrow valleys below, and of the streams which far away in the depths one can hear wending their way over their rocky beds to join the larger rivers which drain the lower lands. We have heard of the feelings

of wonder with which the traveller realizes the fact
that the constant dripping of the water has worn
away enormous quantities of rock, and has assisted
the rushing rivers below to excavate and carve out the
mighty cañons at whose feet they now flow. It seems
almost humorous to say that I saw the same process
going on in a prosaic English town, but such in
miniature it really was. Felixstowe has only recently
given birth to its first local board, and much work therefore remains to be done. In the centre of the town a
road leads from the upper portion to that below the
cliffs. From a visitor's point of view the road is kept
very badly, or rather not kept at all. The result has
been that the showers of many years, descending on the
soft, porous, sandy soil, have excavated a number of
small river-courses, and their beds have been gradually deepened until now some of them make quite
respectable rivers after a fall of rain. One of these
I noticed, which had its source in a young waterfall.
At the point of the fall, I presume, the soil must have
been of a more yielding character than higher up, and
thus in years gone by the water had begun to carve
out a river-bed for itself. This process had gone on
until a depth of about four feet had been excavated,
simply by the falling of the water, and by the strength
given to it by the velocity acquired in descending
from a higher level. The process of carving out a
miniature cañon had then begun, and now the waterfall had receded some distance from where it

evidently commenced operations. Thus it appeared to me that this precipitous chasm in the road, down which, by-the-bye, it was decidedly dangerous to travel after nightfall, presented the principal features in miniature of one of the mighty cañons of Mexico.

The country around Felixstowe is exceedingly pretty, and the botanist will find many rare plants in the vicinity. Of the living objects on the seashore, the small compound animal *flustra* of course is very common, and is often mistaken for a seaweed. Corallines of various species abound, whilst here and there, under the rocks, we see the green and red anemones with their gorgeous flower-like plumes. The visitor to the seaside need never waste an hour, for whilst engaged in the pursuit of Nature he can be successfully engaged at the same time in the pursuit of health.

CHAPTER XV.

A PIECE OF SANDSTONE.

Sermons and stones—Books and brooks—What is sand?—Milk and water—How granite blocks are worn down to sand—Consolidated by iron oxide—The Coral Rag of Oxfordshire—A reptilian bird.

WHAT about a piece of sandstone? There surely cannot be much to interest one in so common a thing as this; we can pick up stones almost anywhere around us. We know very well that some are very hard, whilst others are so fragile that they crumble away as we handle them into a thousand thousand grains of sand. But we do not see much in it to entertain us. We who have to work to provide both for ourselves and for others, have little time to inquire into the why and wherefore of such a thing as a piece of sandstone.

Well, let me see if I can interest you even in this, and cause you perhaps to regard it in a more favourable manner. Shakespeare says there are sermons to be found in stones, and books in the running brooks.

We shall see presently that brooks have a good deal to do with the shaping of stones, in the same way that books have a great deal to do with the shaping and formation of modern sermons, so that Shakespeare's analogy has perhaps far more depth of meaning than we are accustomed to see in it.

All holiday-keepers have experienced the pleasurable sensation of walking over the beautiful crisp sands at our various seaside towns, and perhaps have wondered what it is that goes to make sand. You take a handful, and watch it trickling between your fingers, forming as it falls to the ground little hillocks or miniature mountains. You at once observe that it is made up of innumerable grains so tiny that it is difficult to say, See, I have a single grain of sand. Now, all these grains must have had an origin. In all probability the mass of sand is of a greenish tint, although you will occasionally see little black specks which at once show that all the grains are not alike in colour, or in composition. Perhaps tiny fragments of a mineral known as *mica* have become mixed with the greenish sand, having been derived from what are known as primitive rocks, whose cliffs have been beaten and thrashed by the waves in those localities where they form the coast, as in Cornwall and Wales. Here they have been compelled to give up their black shining mica, which, when broken up into atoms, has become mixed with our well-known sands. But all these greenish-coloured grains, whence do they come ?

To answer this, we must first of all find out of what they are composed, and then, if we discover a coast of rocks near which contain this mineral, we shall not be far wrong in attributing the origin of the sand to these rocks. Let us take, for instance, the sands at Brighton. Now the coast here consists of cliffs of chalk. The chalk is intersected both upwards and across by bands of flints. Flints also occur throughout the mass in the form of nodules. If we were to chemically examine the sand we should find that it was composed almost entirely of a mineral called *silex*, which is a compound of silicon and oxygen. But flint, when examined, is found also to consist of silex; therefore flint and sand are chemically the same, the only difference being an apparent one. The flint contains the material of some millions of grains of sand chemically precipitated, and it may consequently be crushed artificially, and be made to produce sand. The sand will naturally not be quite pure silex, as while the flints are being washed out of the chalk to form sand, the chalk at the same time suffers erosion, and its grains, which are not sand (or silex), will be mixed with the sand. It seems strange that the chalk grains are not more intermingled with the sand. But at the base of the cliffs to the east of Brighton, at high tide, the water will be seen to assume a milky appearance owing to the presence of the chalk. This source is, however, not drawn upon for the milk-supply of town (as someone may perhaps suggest).

Chalk and flint beds do not, however, occur everywhere on our coasts. Whence comes, for instance, the sand of such granite districts as Cornwall? Why, from the granite itself. There we find hundreds of rivers, streams, and brooks, all wending their way seawards. Each river and stream wears the surface of the granite pebble-bed over which it flows. Sometimes large blocks are carried down by the currents, and, knocked and tossed about against each other, are ground down at last to powder. Follow the course of such a block. See it start as an angular fragment of granite. Watch its progress and note its continual diminution in size. Also note particularly that all its angular edges are broken off, and ask if such a rounded, water-worn boulder is the same that started on its seaward course from the Cornish granite height. I . have sometimes found such a rounded piece of granite on the Brighton beach itself, washed up the channel from some primitive district by the tides and currents. What has become of these ground-down fragments? They have been borne seawards, have perhaps formed the sand in the beds of streams, and have been used, in a similar manner to that in which we use emery-powder, to further the work of polishing the stones in the beds of rivers whilst being carried forward by the current. Granite is a highly silicated mineral. Of its components, felspar, quartz, and mica, felspar often contains as much as 65 per cent. of silica, mica never less than 40 per cent.,

8

while quartz is, as is well known, the purest form of silex known. Thus we see that quartz and flint are of identical composition. We have, therefore, in granite all the necessaries to form sand.

In examining the contents of the beds of the various streams which intersect Dartmoor, I found these constituents of granite in every size and shape. One little pool at the side of a stream was banked up in the direction of the flow of the current so that the water which it received did not escape directly. Here the matter held in suspension had been deposited. Little pebbles, some more rounded, some less rounded, were intermingled with fine sand. Sometimes in these quiet pools stones of value are found, such as the garnet, tourmaline, Derbyshire-spar, and iron pyrites. These 'accessory' minerals are therefore occasionally found in the granite, although of course forming but an insignificant portion of it. They contain a large percentage of silica, and are in time worn down to a fine sand.

Our piece of sandstone, however, has by some means or other become agglomerated into a compact mass. We must therefore examine some of the various agencies which are at work consolidating sand into hard sandstone. Extreme pressure is perhaps as potent an agent as any. The most consolidated sandstone is always loose enough to enable us to scratch grains therefrom. Flint has been deposited by chemical agencies in the past, and is seen now undergoing chemical deposition in many hot-water springs. Sandstone on the other hand is the mere mechanical agglomeration and consolidation of grains of sand. This consolidation is brought about often by the percolation of an acid through its mass. The continual dribbling through sand of water charged with the peroxide of iron, whilst hardening it, changes the whole of its aspect. All have doubtless noticed the red sands south of Red Hill, from which the town derives its name. These have been coloured by the oxide of iron; iron sandstone, or ironstone, as it is called, being plentiful in Surrey and Sussex. There are some inland beds of sand which have been found broken through by a volcanic dyke. Where this has happened, the sand has undergone a strange metamorphism. The heat of the protruding mass of fiery matter from below has changed the adjacent sandstone into a shining chert-like substance. The action has in some cases altered the aspect of the fossils found in the bed in a similar manner. It is especially noticeable in beds of the Coral Rag, a secondary formation, in which fossil corals are abundant.

Thus we have seen how a piece of sandstone has originated and of what it is composed. Sandstones are not all of the same degree of fineness. A bed occurs in the Coal formation which is largely drawn upon for the supply of millstones and grinding stones. It is called the Millstone Grit, a grit being a sandstone in which the particles measure, perhaps, 1-16th of an inch square, and are plainly visible to the naked eye.

Other sandstones occur which are very finely grained. Such an one is the Lithographic Sandstone of Germany. This is largely used for lithographic printing, owing to the fact that a section presents a naturally even surface, the grains being so small that they are, singly, almost invisible.

This Lithographic Sandstone is the geologists' paradise. It has yielded innumerable very important animal remains. This is almost what we might have expected, the fine sedimentary deposit taking the imprint of remains imbedded in it with faithful certainty. In it have been found the remains of that half-bird, half-reptile, *Archæopteryx*, which are to be seen in the Natural History Museum at South Kensington.

Can I then say in conclusion that a sandstone has some elements of interest in it? Perhaps my reader will look in future a little more kindly on the dry stone which he treads beneath his feet, even though after all it be but a piece of sandstone.

CHAPTER XVI.

A FEW FACTS ABOUT THE ROMAN WALL ROUND LONDON.

London in Cæsar's time—Its early trade—The Wall—When built—Tiles, sandstone and cement—To be built into the new Post Office buildings—Other fragments.

RECENT excavations in the neighbourhood of St. Martin's-le-Grand have brought to light an exceptionally fine portion of the old London Wall, which once surrounded the city of London; and considerable interest has been manifested in this relic, fifteen hundred years old, of the time when Britain owned the almost universal sway of Rome.

To call to mind the Lun-don, or Lyndon, of the time of Julius Cæsar's second invasion in 54 B.C., we must imagine a Celtic hill-fortress on Tower Hill, with extensions, perhaps, as far as Cornhill and Ludgate; to the north a wide extent of moor and marsh, covered in great part by a thick forest, affording ample protection from hostile tribes, at a time when Moorfields was really what its name implies, and when the stream of Wall-brook flowed along the western boundary of the city, while farther west the Fleet river, flowing on the present site of Faringdon Street, poured its navigable waters into Father Thames at Blackfriars. Even as early as the reign of Augustus, British merchants are mentioned by Strabo as trading with the merchants of the Seine and Rhine, in dogs, iron, and other products; so that while Cæsar found Britain to a great extent in a state of savagery, he also found that in certain towns she had advanced somewhat in the paths of civilization, as evinced by her trade with foreign parts.

The Romans withdrew from Britain about A.D. 448, this giving about 500 years as the length of their stay. There is no doubt that under Roman sway Britain advanced rapidly towards civilisation, and, adopting the advice which Agricola gave on the completion of his conquest of Britain, viz., to study the arts of peace, London, then Londinium, laid the basis of her subsequent greatness by drawing to herself the commerce of the nations. Tacitus, in A.D. 62, tells us that Londinium was highly celebrated for the number of its merchants and the wealth of its commerce.

It was not, however, until the fourth century that the great Roman wall was built. Constantine the Great is said to have reared it, and also to have christened London by the name of Augusta, in honour of his mother. The walls were afterwards repaired by

Theodosius, and London became one of the first of the seventy Roman cities of Britain. They were also subsequently repaired by Alfred the Great, when he had regained possession of the city after its sack by the Danes.

According to Pennant, the wall was more than three miles in circumference, twenty-two feet high, and possessed forty lofty towers. Commencing at the river on the east side of the Tower, the wall took a north-westerly course, up the Minories to the Ealdgate, or old-gate (Aldgate); it then continued by Houndsditch to Bishopsgate, where, turning due west, it followed the direction of London Wall to St. Giles's Church, Cripplegate. Turning south for a short distance, the wall ran to Falcon Square, whence again running to the west, it crossed Aldersgate, and arriving at New-gate, turned southward through the old Bailey to the river.

The section recently exposed at St. Martin's-le-Grand is now in the finest state of preservation, and is situate in that portion of the wall running between Falcon Square and Newgate. Its site can easily be fixed by those who remember the French Protestant Church in Aldersgate Street, since the wall ran immediately beneath the church. Standing at the end of the section, and looking easterly along its direction, it is seen to pass immediately under the party-wall which divides the two houses on the oppo-site side of the street, on one of which appears the street-name 'Aldersgate Street,' while on the other appears 'St. Martin's-le-Grand.' This, then, marks the site of the old 'Alders-gate,' the one house being now, doubtless, in a separate parish from that of the other.

The wall exposed is about fourteen feet in height, the upper portions having been removed to make room for cellars, etc., which were seen to be resting upon it.

On a foundation of a foot and a half of ragstone, irregularly hewn, rested a double layer of red tiles to a thickness of about five inches. On these was a thickness of three feet of regularly-hewn sandstone blocks, from a foot to a foot-and-a-half in length by eight inches in height. Immediately above was another layer of red tiles, similar in character to the previous layer, and again succeeding this was a thickness of about $2\frac{1}{2}$ feet of sandstone blocks. In the same way tiles again followed, covered again by sandstone. Altogether five layers of tiles were noticeable, although the two uppermost had been considerably disturbed by building operations. At each layer of tiles it was observed that advantage had been taken to set back the succeeding blocks of sandstone, so that looking from above, the set-off in the height of 14 feet was about $1\frac{1}{2}$ feet. The thickness of the wall at the base was said to be 15 feet.

The tiles were $1\frac{1}{2}$ inches thick, 18 inches long, and 12 inches wide, placed alternately with their long and short edges to the face of the wall.

The cement consisted of lime, sand, small gravel, and a sprinkling of powdered tile. The wall ran almost parallel to what was formerly Bull and Mouth Street. This street, as is well known, has been entirely removed to clear a space for the new buildings in connection with the Post Office. In a book published in 1823, the name of the street is said to have been derived from the old Boulogne Mouth Inn, which formerly stood in the street. In accordance with the way in which the name was pronounced, this was soon corrupted to 'Bull and Mouth' Inn, and hence the name of the street. It is noteworthy that the wall ends abruptly at the western boundary of the parish of St. Botolph Within, whilst that which extended into the parish of Christ Church had been removed for the excavation of deep cellars.

Fragments of the Roman Wall are still to be seen in other places, but having generally been built into recent walls they are not always accessible to the public. A fragment can be seen at the graveyard of Saint Alphège, in London Wall, almost entirely, however, covered with ivy; in 1852 a piece was built into some stables on Tower Hill; and remains are to be found behind the houses in the Old Bailey. In Thames Street a recent excavation showed that beneath the foundation of hewn sandstone was to be found a layer of chalk and stones, while these in turn were supported by oaken piles, driven doubtless into the soft mud of the water's edge.

While the front of the wall everywhere presented a somewhat even surface, the interior was filled up by large blocks of irregular sandstone rubble, the crevices being filled up by the mortar or cement previously mentioned.

The old Roman city, then, extended from Ludgate in the west to the Tower in the east, a distance of about a mile, whilst from north to south it extended from London Wall to the river, a distance of about half a mile.

The relic of Roman times known as ' London Stone ' situated in Cannon Street, in the wall of Swithin's Church, is supposed by some authorities to be the central milestone from which the various roads to different parts of the Kingdom were measured; this supposition is borne out by the fact that the distances hence to the old Roman stations in many cases coincide with each other.

The first Roman wall and the less known one, for there were two, does not include so large an area as that with which we are all more or less familiar. The first had its course on the north along Cornhill and Leadenhall Street, on the east Billiter Street and Mark Lane, on the south Thames Street, and on the west Walbrook. Roman sepulchres have been found in Bow Lane, Moorgate Street, and Bishopsgate Street Within, these having been used as burial grounds, in accordance with Roman sanitary law, which allowed of such places only outside the city. In digging for the foundations of the Exchange, a gravel-pit was come upon filled with rubbish, such as broken pottery, old sandals, etc., but no coin was found therein later than the reign of the Emperor Severus, showing that up till the end of the third century the ground was open waste outside the original city. In the next century (the fourth) the second and greater wall was built, most likely by Constantine, and the burial grounds removed to without the Eald-gate and the Tower, or rather where the Tower now is. Some have supposed that the White Tower was built by Julius Cæsar, while others believe it to have been commenced by William I.

The portion of the wall lying at St. Martin's-le-Grand has been examined by numerous antiquarian visitors, and the authorities have been prevailed upon to preserve so perfect a relic of the Roman occupation, by causing it to be built into the wall which will form the northern boundary of the new buildings.

APPENDIX.

THE following table has been prepared in order that the reader who wishes to learn the zoological classification of the creatures which have been dealt with in the foregoing pages may obtain at a glance the information he requires. Commencing with the lowest form of life known, it ascends through the various stages of organisation, culminating finally with the highest and most organised of all.

FAMILIAR NAME.	SCIENTIFIC GENUS, OR FAMILY.	CLASS.	SUB-KINGDOM.	
Amœba	Amœbea	Rhizopoda	I. Protozoa	
Foraminifer (Globigerina)	Foraminifera	,,	,,	
Polycystinæ (in Atlantic ooze)	Radiolaria	,,	,,	
Sponge	Spongillus	Spongida	II. Cœlenterata	
Corallines (polypite)	Sertularia	Hydrozoa	,,	
Dead-men's-fingers	Alcyonidæ	Actinozoa	,,	
Sea-anemone	Actinidæ	,,	,,	
Red coral (polype)	Gorgonidæ	,,	,,	
Massive coral	Madreporidæ	,,	,,	
Starfish	Asteria	Asteroidea	III. Echinodermata	
Sea-urchin	{ Echinus, Diadema }	Echinoidea	,,	
Lily Encrinite	Encrinus	Crinoidea	,,	Invertebrates.
Insects	—	Insecta	IV. Annulosa	
Serpula	Tubicola		,,	
Acorn-shell	Balanus	Crustacea	,,	
Barnacle	Lepas anatifera	,,	,,	
Lobster	Astacus	,,	,,	
Sea-mat (polypide)	Flustra foliacea	Polyzoa	V. Mollusca	
Gribble-worm	Limnorea terebrans	Acephala	,,	
Ship-worm	Teredo navalis	,,	,,	
Whelk, reversed	Fusus contrarius	Gasteropoda	,,	
Scallop	Pecten	Lammelli-branchiata	,,	
Oyster	Ostrea		,,	
Pearl oyster	Meleagrina meangrina	,,	,,	
Cyrena (marble)	Cyrena	,,	,,	
Mussel	Mytilus edulis	,,	,,	
Razor-shells (borers)	Pholas	,,	,,	

FAMILIAR NAME.	SCIENTIFIC GENUS, OR FAMILY.	ORDER.	CLASS.	
Shark, teeth of	Carcharodon	Chondropterygii	Pisces	
Iguanodon, great Wealden reptile	Iguanodon Mantelli	Dinosauria	Reptilia	Vertebrates.
Bird, fossil	Archæopteryx	Saururæ	Aves	
Marsupials, kangaroo, etc.	Macropus, etc.	Marsupialia	Mammalia	
Earbone of whale	Cetotolithes	Cetacea	,,	
Mastodon, fossil elephant	Elephas primigenius	Ungulata (Proboscoidea)	,,	
Man	Homo	Primates	,,	

THE END.

Elliot Stock, Paternoster Row, London.